A Recipe To Die For

Raye De John

BALBOA.
PRESS

A DIVISION OF HAY HOUSE

Balboa Press books may be ordered through booksellers or by contacting:

Balboa Press
A Division of Hay House
1663 Liberty Drive
Bloomington, IN 47403
www.balboapress.com
1 (877) 407-4847

Because of the dynamic nature of the Internet, any web addresses or
links contained in this book may have changed since publication and
may no longer be valid. The views expressed in this work are solely those
of the author and do not necessarily reflect the views of the publisher,
and the publisher hereby disclaims any responsibility for them.

The author of this book does not dispense medical advice or prescribe
the use of any technique as a form of treatment for physical, emotional,
or medical problems without the advice of a physician, either directly
or indirectly. The intent of the author is only to offer information
of a general nature to help you in your quest for emotional and
spiritual well-being. In the event you use any of the information in
this book for yourself, which is your constitutional right, the author
and the publisher assume no responsibility for your actions.

Any people depicted in stock imagery provided by Thinkstock are
models, and such images are being used for illustrative purposes only.
Certain stock imagery © Thinkstock.

Printed in the United States of America.

ISBN: 978-1-4525-2116-9 (sc)
ISBN: 978-1-4525-2117-6 (e)

Balboa Press rev. date: 10/3/2014

I would like to thank
my daughter Lea for encouraging me to write

Special thanks
to
Tony and Sandy Parente
for their
generosity

Contents

A Recipe to Die For

Janelle was checking each table, to make sure the place settings were perfect. The fragrance of the fresh cut flowers filled the air as she arranged them in their color-coordinated vases. She wanted everything in her restaurant to be impeccable, and pleasing, to the eye; after all, The Sandbox was a very popular meeting place for the intellectuals of the local college. On any given night celebrities, from movie stars to visiting royalty, would stop in to dine and visit with her. Not only did she have the reputation for serving culinary delight, but it also took a lot of hard work and attention to small details to make it the number one restaurant in the affluent town of Crestview, California.

The Sand Box was perfectly located on the tip of the peninsula; about three hundred yards from the blue, crystal clear Pacific Ocean with a magnificent panoramic view of sun baked shores topped with white-capped waves.

She attributed the restaurant's success not only to the excellent cuisine, but also the spectacular sunsets. It was a very pleasant experience, to be dining on her sumptuous veal, sautéed in Marsala wine, while watching the slowly sinking sun turn the sky from blue to pink to crimson. Then, almost by magic, the vivid colors turned into a deep blue that looked almost black. To see the brilliant silver stars, reminiscent of shimmering diamonds, slowly fill up the sky, was a breathtaking, magnificent sight.

Such a lazy day, she thought as she looked out from the floor to ceiling windows at the flock of seagulls circling over some dead fish that had been washed up onto the shore. Her soft brown eyes took on a glazed expression as her lovely face became frozen in time; for once again, she slipped into the same old daydream of being on an adventure in some far away land.

Quiet often she felt herself drifting from this world into her own private place where she had gone so many times before. Ever since she was a child, starting at the early age of seven, when she created this personal universe where no one was allowed to enter and possibly hurt her.

Janelle blamed her daydreams on all the books she had consumed early on in her lonely life. Every precious free moment she had, was spent reading, living her life vicariously through books and the adventures of others, real or imagined.

As far back as she could remember she was always alone. When she was able to fend for herself her mother would put a book in her hands and tell her to look at the pictures, because she was just too ill to play with her.

Janelle's mother Beatrice, a striking looking woman in her day, with her thick curly red hair and large hazel eyes, was always sick. She spent most of her life in a darkened bedroom suffering with migraine headaches. Of course, Janelle took full responsibility for her mother's illness, since it started the day she was born, a week after her mom had just turned seventeen.

Before Beatrice became pregnant with Janelle, she had dreamed of going to Hollywood to become a famous movie star. Acting was her true love. As a small child, she would dress up in her mother's clothes and high heel shoes and stand before a mirror pretending she was someone famous.

Beatrice was always chosen for the best roles in the school plays. Once she had the part of Laura Wingfield, a fragile girl with a limp, from the play The Glass Menagerie by Tennessee Williams. She was brilliant in the part and became her character so thoroughly that she walked with a limp for a month after the play was over.

People were constantly telling her that she was a natural born actress and one day her name would be in lights all over Hollywood. She believed that she was destined for fame and fortune. Beatrice even had a stage name picked out; it was going to be Janelle. Every waking moment she would fantasize of being pursued by adoring fans and attending press parties, with every reporter vying for her attention.

Beatrice's parents were against all this nonsense of becoming a movie star and were slightly relieved when she starting dating the handsome popular Tommy Conner. Her father believed Tommy possessed all the important qualities for a perspective son-in-law. Not only was Tommy tall and very good looking with his coal black hair, he also had a very charming, although a somewhat shy personality for a muscular tough looking football player. He was so good at the game that all his friends were betting that he was a shoe in for an athletic scholarship to Notre Dame.

Tommy had a part-time job as a clerk, in the law firm of Liebowitz and O'Donnel. The lawyers in the office encouraged him to study law by giving him old law books in exchange for his helping them with research on their current cases. Tommy told Beatrice that he was toying with the idea of becoming a judge. He was obsessed with the thought of sitting on the bench gavel in hand fully in charge over the lives of others the idea of so much power fascinated him.

His favorite pastime was sitting in a courtroom listening to the lawyers presenting their cases. He would constantly refer to the stack of law books by his side for reference. Actually he was secretly studying the movements of the magnificent eloquent judges in their wonderful black robes.

On Saturday nights he would take Beatrice to all the movies that were about courtroom trials. She didn't care, as long as she could pretend that it was she on the screen and not Lana Turner.

When Beatrice became pregnant, her parents and Tommy's forced them to get married. When their daughter was born, Beatrice gave her the stage name she so adored... Janelle. Therefore, every time she looked at her little girl, it was a constant reminder of her lost dream.

So with the birth of Janelle, two lives were crushed. Beatrice's love for the movies was out of her head, but not ever.... out of her heart. Tommy took a job at the local factory and began drinking about the same time that Beatrice's migraine headaches started, right after the birth of their only child.

Consequently Janelle never knew love or harmony in her home, only indifference and violence. When her father was upset because the dinner was not what he wanted, or the house wasn't clean enough, he would scream at her mother, break the dishes and storm out of the house leaving the disaster of his anger for someone else to clean up and make right. Whenever Janelle would see her father's rage start, she would quietly leave the room and hide either in the corner of the closet, eyes closed tight, hands over her ears, buried in clothes, or in the attic among yesterday's treasures, hiding behind the large trunks.

It was at this time that the daydreams started. In her mind, she would escape her surroundings by becoming one of the characters in whatever book she was reading. Her favorite was Alice in Wonderland. She would picture herself sipping tea with the Mad Hatter, or giggling with the white rabbit. Then slowly from afar, after her father's storm was over, she would hear her mother calling her name and reluctantly, Janelle would return to reality.

As a child, she never played after school with any of her friends, for fear it would disturb her sick mother. Buried deep down inside her, she knew it really wasn't because of her mother. She didn't want any of her friends to see her father drunk. It wasn't that she was ashamed of him she just didn't want them to make fun of her dad. So out of loneliness she turned to the only other person besides her family with whom she felt comfortable, her next-door neighbor Mary. She was a little, gray haired widow in her mid fifties, with a heart that overflowed with kindness towards Janelle.

It seemed that Mary bonded with Janelle because she reminded her of her childhood and vowed that no child should be ignored or made to feel worthless. She was lucky enough to have married a wonderful man and together they shared five years of total bliss, until he suddenly died of a brain tumor. She didn't ask God why, or moan about not being blessed with any children, that wasn't Mary's style. She simply thanked him for giving her five good years.

Mary looked out the window at Janelle sitting on the stairs and felt sorry for the lonely girl. It seemed that this child was always isolated from the other children. Mary recalled that even when Janelle was a baby, she was left to play alone in her sandbox.

Tears started welling up in Mary's eyes as she looked at the solemn looking child. She wiped her eyes, stepped out onto the porch, waved to her and said, "Janelle, why don't you come over and I'll teach you how to cook a marvelous Italian meal for your father and mother."

Janelle's eyes lit up with excitement as she jumped down from the stairs and ran over to Mary's house. This wonderful woman completely changed her life with this kind gesture. Not only did Mary teach her how to cook many tasty dishes, but also it was the woman's friendship that Janelle treasured through the years. Mary was the mother Janelle never got to know.

"First things first," said Mary, "remember the hands must always be clean, so wash up and I'll tell you what to do next." Janelle beamed with delight. This was the very first meal she was going to cook all by herself and she was so excited. She hurriedly washed her hands with a lot of soap, rinsed them thoroughly, wiped them dry and rushed back into the kitchen.

"OK Mary, what do I do now?" Although it was more than seventeen years ago, it seemed like yesterday and Janelle could still hear Mary's voice guiding her.

"We'll use the large frying pan," she said. "Let's see, we need:

3 tablespoons of olive oil

1 clove of crushed garlic

2 cups of chopped fresh tomatoes

4 leaves of fresh basil

Just a pinch of lemon pepper

"Now turn the flame on low and add the crushed garlic to the warmed oil. Be careful, sometimes it splashes if the oil is too hot. Add the tomatoes and the fresh basil, remember this, Janelle it's always best to use fresh ingredients. Now just stir until the tomatoes are soft and mushy. It's time now for a pinch of lemon pepper."

"Mary, how much is a pinch?" Janelle asked with wide eyes.

"I'll show you honey, it's this much," and Mary picked

up some lemon pepper with her thumb and index finger, "see about half a teaspoon. Next, in a separate pot boil one pound of pasta until soft, drain and put in a large bowl and pour the cooked tomatoes over the pasta. Sprinkle some grated Parmesan cheese on top, and add just a sprig of parsley, to make it look pretty. Remember, the food always tastes better when you make it look pretty. Now take it to your mama, while it's still nice and hot."

Janelle ran home and set the bowl on the table just as her father walked into the house from work. As usual his head was bent, his shoulders sagged she thought he looked so sad. To her surprise she watched him sniff the air and with a smile, he would say, "What smells so good?"

She was delighted as she ran for some plates and forks. "Mary taught me how to cook and I made this all by myself," as she beamed with pride.

"This is wonderful," he said, and for the first time, her father smiled at her as he ate with great gusto.

That is when she discovered how to pacify him. She would hurry home from school, clean the house and run over to Mary's. Over the years, Mary taught her how to cook many wonderful dishes. Her father would eat, drink his wine and just pass out without destroying anything.

Sometimes, in those rare sober moments when he was sitting in the living room reading his old law books while sipping his coffee, he would look at her and tell her that she was so pretty and sweet. Then he would cry and she knew she was the cause of his sorrow. The guilt she felt was overpowering, she knew it had to be her fault that her father's dreams were crushed.

To escape the pain of so much guilt, she would turn to her books. While reading a story about Egypt, it wasn't the character in the book riding on that camel through the desert on an adventure, it was she and she would feel alive. Janelle swore that when she became eighteen, she would travel the world and leave behind all this misery. It didn't matter what her life was like now. Janelle was more interested in what it was going to be like and would surrender to her imagination and slip into yet another daydream.

Veal Marsala

1 pound of boneless veal cutlets, pounded thin.
$\frac{1}{4}$ cup flour
3 tbs. of butter or margarine
$\frac{1}{2}$ tsp. salt, dash pepper
1 $\frac{1}{2}$ cup thinly sliced mushrooms
2 tbs. of butter or margarine
2 tbs. flour
$\frac{1}{2}$ cup Marsala wine
1-cup chicken broth
Hot cooked Rice, or noodles.

Slice veal into 2" x $\frac{1}{2}$" strips. In a sturdy plastic bag, place veal and $\frac{1}{4}$ cup flour. Shake to coat evenly. In an electric skillet, melt 3 tbsp of butter with heat control set at 325 degrees. When the butter is bubble, add veal strips. Sauté quickly, until all sides are brown. Sprinkle with salt and pepper. Remove veal from skillet. Keep warm. Add mushrooms to hot skillet and Sauté, until limp. Add 2 tbsp butter and 2 tsp flour, stirring well to combine. Add wine and broth, stirring constantly to loosen any brown bits, for 2 minutes. Add veal and simmer for 1 minute or until heated through. Serve over rice or noodles if desired, makes 4 to 5 servings.

The Letter

Janelle sighed and shook herself back to the present. She could cope with the daydreams, they weren't bad, but she shuddered when she thought of the recent terrifying nightmares that sent chills through her.

She turned as she heard the door of the restaurant open, and greeted Harry, the postman, a welcomed diversion from her thoughts.

"Hi Harry, how many bills do you have for me today?"

"None," he replied. "But I do have a registered letter for you from New Orleans."

"New Orleans?" Her curiosity was peaked, could it be from him? Her heart skipped a beat just thinking about him. Even after all these years she felt this strange tingling sensation go through her body whenever she pictured his handsome face. Impossible! Wake up girl, you have not seen or heard from him in several years. You pushed him away, remember?

"Aren't you going to open it?

"Not now, first how about some breakfast on the house?"

"It's always on the house. I swear Janelle you're too kind hearted to be a businesswoman. Yes, I do want breakfast," Harry sighed, as he set his heavy mailbag down on the table closest to the kitchen. "I've been dreaming about those wonderful peaches and pecan waffles that only you can make, but I will pay for it," as he rubbed his sore shoulder.

Janelle smiled for she knew that when Harry made up his mind about something there wasn't anything she could say or do to change it. She poured a cup of coffee and gave him the paper to read while she prepared his waffles.

"I sure wish my wife could cook," he said wistfully. "I love her dearly but she is terrible at it. I married her for her many other qualities, "he smiled, "but cooking is not one of them. Say Janelle, do you think that you could give her some lessons?"

"For you Harry, you bet. I'll print out the recipe for her and if she has any questions, tell her to call me or stop in. You know I'm always here."

She busied herself in the kitchen making his waffle. It took all of ten minutes and it looked luscious. She served it to Harry and with his mouth full he said, "Please Janelle, I'm begging you to teach my wife how to make this. I promise I'll be beholden to you forever."

She laughed and walked over to her computer printed the recipe and handed it to him. He nodded as he took the last sip of his coffee and said, "This really was the best waffle I've ever tasted. You know, I was just marveling at how different the restaurant looks now, than it did when it was called Jake's Place. You really made some major changes in the past two years since you've owned it," he commented as he walked around the room and gently touched his very favorite white marble statue. It was of two lovers kissing tenderly, that Janelle had brought back from Genoa. "Your restaurant is undeniably quite attractive now," he said as he picked up his heavy mailbag. "Well I've got to go. Break time is over," and he handed her the money.

"Ok Harry, if you insist." She rang up the check on the

register and handed him the change. "You have a nice day and try to stay out of the way of any mean dogs," she said as he laughed and walked out the door. Janelle picked up the letter that she had left on the counter and shoved it deep in her pocket, almost as if she were afraid to open it. "Later," she mumbled. "I'll open it later."

She removed Harry's dishes and finished checking her tables. As she looked around, she realized that Harry was right. When she first went to work at Jake's Place it was just a diner with old chrome and red plastic upholstered chairs. The gray tile floor was always covered with a fine mist of sand. After a few major changes, the restaurant became quite elegant and attractive. The patches of wall between the windows were covered in white silk moiré with matching upholstered chairs. The floors and tabletops were all white marble with veins of light beige running through them. The table and chair legs were white washed wood, almost the color of the veins in the marble. The one point that made this restaurant so different from others was not only the combination of silk moiré and marble; which gave off an elegant look. It was that each table was individually decorated with fresh flowers that coordinated to enhance the matching antique place settings and crystal goblets. Consequently her customers would call and reserve a table by color. She knew that certain patrons always wanted the purple table while others the yellow table, etc. The different patterned and shaped dishes made her customers feel special. Janelle had thrown herself into every small detail of the restaurant. She loved being busy. It took her mind off of her loneliness.

Her staff was starting to arrive. Soon she would be absorbed in the business of running the restaurant, too occupied to think about her letter, while deep within the recesses of her mind, she hoped, it was from him.

Peaches and Pecan Waffles

2 cups of sifted flour
2 tbsp sugar
3 tsp of baking powder
2 eggs separated
1 tsp salt
1-½ cups of milk
6 tbsp canola oil

Sift together all dry ingredients. Beat egg yokes, than add milk and oil. Pour into flour mixture and stir just enough to moisten dry ingredients. Fold in egg whites, which have been beaten until stiff but not dry. Grease a hot waffle iron and pour batter to one inch from edge. Bake 4 to 5 minutes.

The Topping

3 fresh ripe peaches
½ cup of brown sugar
½ cup of pecans
3 drops of Cream De Cocoa

Rub fuzz from peaches with a clean cloth, wash and cut into thin slices. Add chopped pecans, and brown sugar. Place in a microwavable bowl and cover with plastic wrap. Microwave for 3 minutes and add Cream De Cocoa, mix well and pour over cooked waffle.

The Beginnings

Business was very good, possibly due to the upcoming holidays. With Christmas only a few weeks away, the college would be closed for a month and everyone was in a party mood. She stepped into the kitchen and saw her old neighbor and best friend Mary overseeing the entire operation, giving order to everyone at once. The woman is extraordinary, thought Janelle; even at the age of seventy-two she is still very active.

Janelle could tell by the way Mary walked that her legs were hurting her, probably because of the moisture from the ocean. She needed a drier climate and Janelle was going to surprise Mary and Sally by giving them a vacation in Las Vegas as a Christmas present. Trying to make her rest was just impossible, although Mary was hurting, she was just so thankful she was needed. The job gave her an excuse as she put it, to get up in the morning; and Janelle had never seen her so happy.

"Mary, please calm down," said Janelle. "Come sit and rest with me. Let's have a cool drink and some peace and quiet in my office. The rush hour is almost over and as usual you've done a superb job."

"Janelle honey, wait just a minute, let me fix this plate of salmon. It needs some thinly sliced curled cucumbers, one over-lapping the other, with a slight dribble of balsamic vinegar and olive oil. There now, doesn't that look better?"

"Yes Mary, as usual you're right. Now it looks pretty," as the picture flashed through her mind of the first cooking lesson Mary had given her so many years ago.

"You must promise to never leave me," Janelle said as her eyes misted up with tears. "I'd simply be lost without you."

Mary's round body shook with laughter, "Leave you? Heck no, I'm having too much fun. I'm afraid you're stuck with me honey." They both laughed and you could see the love between them was unconditional.

Sally the waitress, also a long time friend, entered the kitchen asking for her plate of salmon. Janelle handed her the plate and asked her to please join them in her office for a cool drink as soon as she could. "I'll be there in five minutes," said Sally as she hurried off to serve her last customer.

Janelle kicked off her shoes as she entered her office. It felt so good after standing all day. She always loved walking barefoot, especially in the sand at the water's edge.

She sat down at her desk and started to remember the first day she came to this building, when it was called Jake's Place. It all seemed so long ago. She remembered she was deep in thought and worried about conditions at home. She had been walking barefoot in the cool water, feeling the sand squishing through her toes, after each wave receded back out to sea.

They had very little groceries left, the rent was due in two weeks and a total of only twenty dollars was in the drawer. She looked up as if to ask the heavens for help, when she noticed the restaurant at the tip of the peninsula. A determined look came upon her face, as she brushed the sand off her feet, put her shoes on and determinedly walked toward the restaurant to beg the owner Jake, for a job.

She was so desperate to work, that she lied about her age. She told Jake she was seventeen and knew all about waitress work. He just shook his head, knowing she was lying, but as he looked at her, he noticed that desperate stubborn look on her face, and said; "Sure why not, your hired."

Those were the sweetest words she ever heard, YOU'RE HIRED. She ran home to tell her mom that she got a job. Now, she thought, everything would be all right. Her father's drinking had gotten worse and half the time his paycheck would get lost to liquor. She was only sixteen and a half to have so much responsibility placed on her shoulders.

Janelle quickly learned all the short cuts of being a good waitress, thanks to another angel looking out for her by the name of Sally. From day one Janelle and Sally were good friends and one would always help out the other during the busy hours.

Sally taught her more than how to carry plates and keep the orders straight. She also showed her how to handle the rich college boys that tried to get fresh with her. Sally invariably had a smart remark whenever her male customers would get out of hand, but always in a friendly kidding way. Although she claimed to be the unluckiest person when it came to men, you would always find her with an admirer or two hanging around.

Sally was in her early forties, tall, thin, blond and pretty, with never a loss for a smart comeback that had everyone roaring with laughter.

When word got around the college, that a new waitress started working at Jake's Place, the restaurant experienced a rush of business. When first meeting Janelle, you noticed a spirit about her that was difficult to describe. Perhaps it was the way she stood with her shoulders back and her head held high, or the way she had of looking straight into your eyes whenever she spoke to you. Her voice was very soft and her words so genuine and sincere, you had to be very careful in her presence; it was very easy to get lost in the warmth of her soft brown eyes.

Although Janelle is attractive, she was not the most beautiful girl in the world. I guess you could describe her as magnetic. When walking into a room full of strangers, she instantly would find herself surrounded by both men and women craving her attention. She was just a friendly warm sensitive person with genuine kind feelings, a kindred spirit.

You may attribute this magnetism to her daydreams of the life she wanted which captured her excitement for living. People around her felt this energy and quite often after speaking with Janelle, this aliveness encompasses them, and they were never the same. It was as if an invisible force entered them, and they too felt the need to live life to its fullest, to make each day count.

It was this quality about her that made the restaurant so successful. She quite simply was unforgettable. Whenever life became wearisome or mundane, people wanted to feel the electricity of Janelle's presence.

Lately, it seemed, Jake's Diner was always packed. The waiting line went around the building. "Sally is it always this busy?" Janelle asked.

"Only, since you started working here. Everyone wants to see the new beautiful red haired waitress."

Janelle shrugged her shoulders and thought Sally was just kidding her for never in a million years, did she ever consider herself beautiful. She didn't even think she was pretty.

When Janelle went home that night, she took a long hard look in the mirror. She would see her image entirely different than other people would see her. She hated her red hair; it was too curly, too long, too wild looking. Sometimes she would try to wear it straight back for an older more sophisticated look. It never worked, there would always be one long curl that would come loose and fall over her left eye. She would see her nose and think it's too long. Others would see it as a perfectly aristocratic, classically thin nose. She considered her eyes a boring brown, while admirers were amazed at the specks of gold, almost the color of honey, and a smoldering hidden longing for love that was buried very deep within them. For when you looked into Janelle's eyes, you saw her soul.

The knock on the door forced Janelle back to the present. She shook off the reverie of the past, as Mary, Alice and the busboy Pedro entered. Pedro was carrying fresh lemonade for the three of them. He looked handsome in his starched, white jacket as he set the drinks down and left the room. Janelle was glad she took a chance and hired him.

He was a young man that was always in trouble as a teenager and found it difficult to get a job. When Pedro, married his childhood sweetheart Maricella, his life changed for the better. He wanted desperately to leave his old life behind and start a new one. His devotion to Janelle was total, especially since she hired his wife to work part time while their son was in school. She helped him because she could never forget how hard it was to make ends meet when she was young. She even gave him and his wife leftover food to help them along.

While the two women were getting comfortable, Janelle reached for the envelope in her pocket still silently wishing that it were from Beau. As she opened it, an airline ticket fell out onto her desk.

"Are you finally going on vacation?" asked Mary.

"Uh… no," she murmured. "I received this registered

letter today from New Orleans and this is the first chance I have had to open it."

Mary and Sally exchanged glances, as they both said in unison, "New Orleans?"

As she started reading the letter she let out a whopping yell! Mary and Sally jumped to their feet to see what the excitement was all about. The letter was from the New Orleans Greatest Chefs Organization, a very prestigious association.

Janelle read out loud, "You have been selected to be our guest of honor at the New Orleans twenty first convention. It starts December 12th through the 22nd at the Hotel Maison de Ville, located in the French Quarter.

You were chosen as our guest of honor because of your restaurant's creative menu. It has also been brought to our attention that you provide a unique dining experience beautifully displayed on antique dishes. The one meal that really stands out is your succulent pork chop ala apricot dinner. The committee would appreciate a copy of the recipe for the convention.

Enclosed are airline tickets and your confirmation number for the Maison de Ville Hotel. We hope this meets with your approval and once again, congratulations."

Janelle was stunned. She was very familiar with this organization and it was indeed a privilege to have been selected to be guest of honor. Mary and Sally were jumping up and down while tears of joy were streaming down their faces.

"You need a wardrobe, we have to go shopping early tomorrow morning," said Sally excitedly.

"That's right," replied Mary shaking her head up and down. "Tomorrow is Monday and the restaurant is closed. I don't want to hear any excuses. The three of us are headed for Rodeo Drive in Los Angeles. You need some very glamorous clothes for this important occasion."

"Lunch is on me," Sally chimed in. We'll go to The Papagalos Restaurant. It's supposed to be very different. The name means parrot in English and I heard it's a lot of fun. I understand that the restaurant is a hang out for the who's who of Hollywood. Who knows," she said rather dreamily, "maybe I'll meet someone rich and famous who will fall madly in love with me." They all started laughing and dancing around the room with the anticipation of tomorrow.

The next day they went to Rodeo drive, a place like no other in the world. It seemed strange to see elegantly dressed women walking their dogs with leases attached to diamond studded collars. One store in particular sold solid gold gas cans to compliment your Rolls Royce.

They entered into a very posh boutique and were seated on a pink silk sofa, and were served champagne and hors d' oeuvres while clothes were modeled for them.

Mary and Sally insisted Janelle buy several outfits. Among them, a light blue Armani suit, a simple black long dress for the ball, five slack suits for every day use and three dresses for afternoon cocktail parties.

"Janelle you look fabulous in that deep purple dress. She'll take that one too," said Mary to the sales clerk.

Janelle looked at herself in the mirror and smiled. She did like the way it fit. It made her feel pretty and she hadn't felt that way since she and Beau had parted. She shook her head, mustn't think about him, besides, it was such a long time ago.

"Come," said Sally, "it's time for lunch." With their packages in tow they headed for the Papagalos restaurant. Janelle anticipated the usual nice upgraded restaurant, but instead found a wild, crowded, fun place that also served food.

The restaurant was in various shades of white; it looked like a Mediterranean palace. The waiters wore short togas with gold rope belts. The wait, they were informed by this gorgeous man with muscular arms and legs, would be at least 45 minutes. He took their names and directed them to a room where they heard people roaring with laughter.

The room was very large with a bar along one wall that was surrounded by glass, from ceiling to floor. Behind the glass were thousands of parrots, all colors and sizes. Some were all green with yellow beaks, some white or all gray with just a spot of red on the tails and others multicolored. They were magnificent shades of blue, purple, green, red and fuchsia. The bright mix of colors from a thousand parrots was indeed a sight to behold.

"We would like to be seated close to the stage," Sally told the waiter, but before they had a chance to be seated they were joining the crowd with hysterical laughter. Mary was laughing so hard that she couldn't walk a step. Janelle had to grab her arm and guide her to the chair.

On stage was the Maestro, a very distinguished man in his smart looking tuxedo, with a baton in his hand. He was explaining to the audience that he and his parrots were going to perform a medley.

They would sing Maria, 'O paese d'o sole, and Cielito lindo. He had three African gray parrots on three wooden perches along side of him. He tapped his baton for silence then lifted his arms for the music to begin. The parrots cleared their throats and the sound that filled the room was truly marvelous. One by one the parrots began to sing. To everyone's surprise they sounded just like the famous three tenors. It was amazing to hear a wonderful tenor's voice coming from the parrots, but it was also hilarious.

After the show, they were seated for lunch. There wasn't a menu, only one dish was offered. Today they were serving Petti di Pollo ala Bolognese, a delightfully delicious dish.

Janelle smiled as she held Sally and Mary's hands, and said, "This has been a great day, spent with wonderful friends. For the rest of my life, I will always treasure this time we spent together.

Sally and Mary both started wiping away the tears that suddenly appeared and then once again, all three women were laughing hysterically.

Petti Di Pollo Alla Bolognese
(Chicken Breasts with Prosciutto and Cheese)

4 individual chicken breasts, ½ lb each skinned and deboned.
Salt
Freshly ground black pepper
Flour
3 tbsp butter
2 tbsp oil
8 thin, 2″x4″ slices of Prosciutto
8 thin, 2″x4″ slices imported Fontina cheese
4 tsp freshly grated imported Parmesan cheese
2 tbsp chicken stock, fresh or canned

Preheat the oven to 350 degrees. With a very sharp knife, carefully slice each chicken breast horizontally to make 8 thin slices. Season the slices with salt and pepper, then dip them in flour and shake off the excess. In a heavy 12-inch skillet, melt the butter with the oil over moderate heat. Brown the chicken to a light, golden color in the hot fat, 3 or 4 slices at a time. Do not overcook them.

Transfer the chicken breasts to a shallow, buttered baking and serving dish large enough to hold them comfortably. Place a slice of prosciutto and then a slice of cheese on each one. Sprinkle them with grated cheese and dribble the chicken stock over them. Bake uncovered in the center of the oven for about 10 minutes, or until the cheese is melted and lightly browned. Serves four.

Sleep Not, Lest You Dream

It became difficult for Janelle to sleep that night. She thought about Beau Rampart and recalled that day, so many years ago, when he first walked into the diner. Even after all this time whenever she thought of him, her eyes would mist with tears and her heart felt heavy for what could have been.

She recalled it was only her third day on the job and she was trying her best to learn all the tricks of being a good waitress. She was having fun and doing just fine until she looked up and saw this very handsome young man. He was tall, at least 6 foot, with raven black hair. His eyes followed her every move, always with a smile on his face. She was so mesmerized by his looks that she almost dropped two of the dishes. Janelle knew he was from the college and felt intimidated by those students who constantly directed their smart remarks at her.

He sat at a table surrounded by beautiful, well-dressed girls, who were all talking and laughing. She thought for just a moment how wonderful it would be to be so carefree, to wake up each morning without a concern in the world except for keeping up with the latest fashions.

She remembered his face so vividly. Even after six years she could still recall everything about him, from his square jaw, to his deep-set eyes and his habit of always frowning whenever she caught him starring at her. He's so handsome and popular that his presence alone would make her extremely nervous.

She straightened her shoulders, took a deep breath and approached the table, "What would you like?"

"What I would really like is not on the menu," he replied in his quite southern drawl. The sound of his voice invariably made her knees start to buckle. She would catch her breath and try not to look into his piercing, bluish green eyes that were always starring at her. He was gracious and gallant, the perfect southern gentleman; and when he smiled at her she was sure her heart would stop beating. She would roll her eyes toward heaven and silently pray for courage. Janelle was so afraid that she was going to make a complete fool of herself, so before replying, she would take a deep breath and pretend she was Sally.

"Please tell me what you see on the menu that you would like to order. Now, if you're not a fast reader and you need more time, I'll come back when you're ready to order." Oh how she wished she could click her heels together and like Dorothy in the Wizard of Oz and just simply disappear.

His gaze was unnerving. His eyes were filled with wonderment never leaving hers. He stared at her the entire time in the restaurant. Whenever he was around, she tried so hard not to drop any dishes or mix up the orders. It took every bit of concentration she had to just muddle through.

His constant companion was a striking brunette with slightly slanted cold blue eyes. Her name was Mala Maison, and she too was from New Orleans. Her father and Beau's were business acquaintances. When she discovered Beau had enrolled at Crestview College, she informed her father that, she must attend that school. Of course Mala always got what she wanted and, more then anything, Mala wanted

Beau. She could see how this little red haired waitress affected Beau and she didn't like it at all.

One day in particular when the diner was full, she was trying to talk to Beau who just kept staring at Janelle. He watched her every move and whenever he got Janelle's attention, he would smile, and his eyes would light up. Mala became insane with jealousy. She wanted to humiliate Janelle, so she deliberately bumped into her while she s carried a tray full of empty plates. Janelle and the plates went flying, Mala called her a clumsy idiot, loud enough for all her friends to hear and of course start laughing.

"Take my hand Janelle," said Jake as he helped her up."I saw what happened and how that spoiled rotten kid deliberately tripped you. Smile don't give the satisfaction of being hurt or upset, pretend it doesn't bother you, that will make her mad. We will clean up this mess together." He always had a soft spot in his heart for Janelle. She was a good worker and tried so hard to please each and every customer. Jake pushed some extra money into Janelle's hand and told her to take the rest of the day off and not to worry about a few vicious kids.

Shaken and embarrassed, Janelle told herself over and over not to cry. Don't give them the satisfaction. She remembered what Mary always told her; people who are spiteful and petty are just outright mean. They are that way because they feel so miserable inside and want others to feel the same. Just consider the source, forgive them and don't ever let them see you cry.

She thanked Jake for his kindness, slipped out the back door of the restaurant and headed for the beach. Janelle looked forward each day to her quite time, as she called it. This was after work when she could walk barefoot along the water's edge. She wasn't used to standing all day and it always felt so good to feel the cool water and sand on her feet and ankles. It was her time to contemplate. She had been on the job for a few months now and made good money in tips, which made things better financially at home. She was so deep in thought that she didn't realize how high the waves were and how soaked her skirt had become.

The only thing on her mind was rehashing the scene that just occurred in the diner. She could no longer hold back the tears that were streaming down her face. She promised herself that someday she was going to be rich and would never be at the mercy of anyone again. Janelle realized she must have a plan if she was going to achieve success. As she walked along, she contemplated her future and how she wants so much to make something of herself, in spite of her situation. I must go to college, she thought, I just have to find a way. I will never allow anyone to humiliate me again. She wondered if Mala and her friends ever realized how really fortunate they were to have everything in life handed to them; to be living on borrowed wings, so to speak.

Whenever Janelle was faced with a dilemma, she had always turned to Mary for advice. Over the years, it seemed that Mary's words were always there to comfort her. She was trying to think about what Mary always said to her. Oh yes, I remember now, she thought. It was reach for the moon. If you fail, you'll just fall among the stars.

She was going to reach for that moon and someday she would have enough money for stylish clothes like Mala and her friends. And someday she would live in a nice house with beautiful furniture and someday soon, very soon, she was going to be...happy.

Through the roar of the waves she heard someone running behind her. She looked up and saw Beau. He caught up to her and gently took her hand, put it to his lips and kissed her fingers so tenderly.

"Don't cry," he said as he wiped away her tears, and wrapped his arms around her, his manliness just wanted desperately to hold her in his arms, to protect her always.

"In case you haven't noticed Janelle, I'm crazy about you." It was at this moment that he fell madly in love with her. He thought she had to be the most beautiful young woman he had ever seen even with her drenched skirt hugging the outline of her slim thighs. As far as he was concerned, she was perfect. If he could freeze any moment in time, it would be this one. The time that he realized it was Janelle he wanted by his side forever. He knew that somehow, no matter how long it took; he would find a way to spend the rest of his life with her.

She looked up into his eyes and saw that there wasn't any laughter in them only warmth and love. Love so strong, it overpowered her, as she slipped into his arms, so easily and naturally. The moment was so right. She finally felt like she belonged in this universe. For the first time in her life she felt the love of a man touch her. The idea that anyone in the world could have feelings for her was astonishing. What a concept, him holding her so tight, comforting her, it felt wonderful. This was a first and she wished it would last forever, that he would never let go.

They stood on the beach in each other's arms while the waves caressed their bodies with the cool, salt water. At this instant, he wanted to make love to her more than anything in the world but this was not the time or place. He didn't want to spoil their relationship by taking advantage of the vulnerability of the moment. He gently pushed her away from him and kissed her tears from her face. Without a word being spoken, they started walking hand in hand down the beach.

Unbeknownst to them, Mala was observing every move

they made and was filled with rage. She was not going to allow anyone to spoil her plans. Beau was going to marry her, only her, and no little nobody, was not going to get in her way.

The storm loomed just on the horizon. The waves were rushing to the shore with incredible force as the sky lit up with lightning. Rare storm warnings were posted all day, and it looked like it was about to hit with hurricane intensity.

Jake and Sally ran to the outside deck of the diner to secure the umbrellas and tables. As they were tying everything down, the sky lit up again with lightning. That's when Sally noticed Mala standing in the shadow of the porch staring at Janelle and Beau laughing and running hand in hand down the beach as they searched for shelter from the oncoming storm.

Sally shivered as she looked at the young girl's face, so twisted with pure hatred. She knew that the rage that was showing on Mala's face was much more frightening than the awful fury of the storm.

The rain hit suddenly and everyone ran for shelter. Janelle and Beau were so happy they had found each other. It didn't matter if they were soaked to the skin. They were together and that's what was important.

They found refuge under a cliff, sat down on an old log that had been washed up on the beach eons ago, and just held onto each other. With his arms wrapped around her and her body learning back onto him, they talked long into the night about life and their dreams.

Janelle told Beau about her childhood, and how she loved to read book after book about foreign lands. She just knew that someday she would go to all those places she read about. She told him about her family, how worried she was about her father's drinking and how the doctors couldn't find the cause of her mother's terrible headaches.

She talked about her dream of making something of herself and how she longed to be able to attend college. Together they discussed various financial possibilities to attain the money for classes, and how it was very possible to realize your dreams if you just wanted them bad enough.

Beau smiled and savored the shiver that entered his body. He always felt a thrill when something happened to him that was so very right. He thought, finally I found a woman who is not only beautiful and intelligent, but it's so rare to find one who is also a caring loving human being.

Beau told her about his family and how his father was a prominent figure in New Orleans society. His ancestors arrived in Louisiana in the late 17th century. They were fleeing from France during the French Revolution, at a time when their friends were being executed because they came from nobility. His ancestors were able to escape because of the aid that was provided to them by the Comtesse du Barry, the mistress of King Louis XV of France. She sold the jewelry, given to her by the King, to pay for safe passage for Beau's ancestors. She also hid over fifty different families in the dungeons beneath the castle until they could be safely moved. Unfortunately, the Comtesse was not as lucky as all the people she had saved. She was captured by the revolutionaries and guillotined. She had become a martyr and would never be forgotten by the families of those she had aided. It was not uncommon to find her portrait hanging in the homes of the descendants of the families that she had helped.

Out of the swampland, in this new land America, his French Creole old-line ancestors built white, pillared mansions along the banks of the Mississippi, with neat rows of cypress trees leading to the front steps. The sweet, heavy fragrance of gardenias, lavender and night blooming jasmine constantly scented the air.

The entrance hallways were of Italian marble, covering the floors and walls. The magnificently curved stairway was lined with portraits of ancestors from decades past. When in the evening the crystal chandeliers cast their brilliance on the faces of these ancestors, it gave one a sense that these people could never die. Their spirit would always live on from generation to generation.

He told her how the Creole families would hire private chefs from France to cater banquets. These events were called soirees. At least twice a month there would be supper dances for close family and friends with table ladened with exotic dishes. The menus included Shrimp Etoufefee, Creole Gumbo, Jambalaya, Cajun Boudoir sausage, pecan pralines, café' au lait, and beignets, pecan pie, sautéed bananas in brown sugar and red wine.

"Sautéed bananas, I never heard of heating bananas. Do you know how they do that?" Janelle asked with raised eyebrows.

"Now that's the only thing I know how to make because it's my favorite. Every time Delphine, our black Creole cook, would make them I would be sitting in the kitchen helping her." Beau laughed. "Why it would be me and my best friend Etienne, Delphine's son, he's about my age and the two of us were in-separable. We would be sitting at that table slicing bananas as fast as we could. Those were good times for Etienne and me."

"Could you tell me the recipe? I love to cook and this intrigues me."

"Of course, it's really easy."

Janelle filed all the information in the back of her brain

just as she always did whenever she saw, heard, or read something that was interesting to her. She was like a sponge soaking up everything he described. With her eyes closed she envisioned everything. The way the mansion looked with marble walls and floors, the banquet table laden with food.

"Everything on the banquet table was prepared with loving care, said Beau seriously. "Of course, all the food was always elegantly served. It was and still is an exquisite affair. The women in those days wore damask or satin dresses with imported ribbons and lace. The cameos were pinned either on the lace near the throat or above their right breast. From the double parlor or ballroom you could hear music from a small band that was provided for dancing. This tradition is still going on, even today."

Janelle listened to the scene Beau was painting with words. In her mind, she could picture elegantly dressed couples dancing and if she listened really hard, she could hear the music and swishing sound that the women's dresses made while they gracefully moved around the dance floor.

His life was so different than hers. It sounded just like one of her daydreams and to think a measure of this elegance was still part of his world today. She wondered if in time, she would be able to fit into his social circle.

The wind stopped and the rain had dwindled from a downpour to a fine mist. The storm drifted out to sea. The worst was over, but for Janelle and Beau it was a new beginning and the magic of this night would last forever. The stars appeared in the sky and the desolate beach felt like it belonged only to the two of them. They stood up, he held her in his arms and kissed her so tenderly and for a while both of them were lost in the ecstasy of a kiss.

They finally stepped away from each other amazed that

just a few hours could change their lives forever. He walked her home and they stood in front of her house for the longest time talking. There was so much he wanted to know about her, and he knew deep inside his heart that even if she were by his side for the next ten years, he would still feel the same way. Holding her hand tightly he looked deeply into her eyes, trying so hard to memorize every inch of her face. Reluctantly, he stepped back, took her hand to his lips and said goodnight.

Beau tried to analyze what had happened to him tonight. He went from being attracted to Janelle to knowing without a doubt that she was the only one for him. He wanted to hurry home so he could sketch her face from memory.

Although nature's storm ended, the turbulence deep within both Janelle and Beau caused them to spend a lot of sleepless nights yearning for each other.

Bananas Foster

4 tbsp. of butter
1 cup of brown sugar
$\frac{1}{2}$ tsp. of cinnamon
4 tbsp. of banana liquor
$\frac{1}{4}$ cup of rum
4 bananas
4 scoops of vanilla ice cream

Melt butter in a sauté pan; add sugar, cinnamon and banana liquor. Stir to mix. Heat for three minutes, or until barely boiling. Add bananas, cut length wise and quartered to sauce and sauté for one minute.

Add rum and allow to heat well. Ignite mixture; allow burning until flame disappears, while moving pan in a circular motion.

Serve over individual scoops of vanilla ice cream. Serves four.

Mala

"No one", Mala whispered to her full length mirror, "No one takes what I want away from me, and I want, Beau. The first time I saw him was at my stupid cousin Anastasia's coming-out party. She had invited him to be her escort, hah what a joke that was. Klutzy Anastasia didn't deserve to be with someone as handsome as Beau. Well, I nipped that in the bud, that very same night, when I tripped her and she fell into the pool. She was so embarrassed; she didn't go out for a year."

"Now tonight, I will get rid of Janelle once and for all. I thought I would just bide my time and let this little affair run its course. After all, no one in his right mind would take that little redhead instead of me. Now I'm tired of waiting, he has been going with her for two years and tonight it will end."

Beau graduated yesterday, she thought, and he will be heading for New Orleans within the next few days. Once away from Crestview, and after what I have planned for him tonight, we will just see whom he will be dating then.

She kicked a pile of clothes on the floor away from the mirror so she could apply some powder to her face. She put on fresh lipstick, and blotted her lips with a tissue and threw the tissue it on the floor for the maid to clean up. She checked her image from all angles. Every inch of her has to be perfect, from the latest hairdo to her fashionable shoes.

Mala spent hours looking in the mirror every day, totally unconcerned about the lives around her. She was always her main focus. She had her nose shortened, her chin straightened, breast implants, and a few ribs have been removed to give her a slimmer waist. It never entered her mind that perhaps people, who were consumed with themselves, were not mentally stable. Instead of spending time finding ways of helping those less fortunate, she was only concerned with attaining plastic perfection.

She gave herself one last look in the mirror, practiced a few expressions, like looking innocent, sexy and surprised. Perfect, she thought, I really look good. How can anyone, including Beau, resist me? And look good she did. At first glance Mala was a stunning beauty, but when you got to know her, you realized that this was one person to stay away from. Although she was beautiful on the outside, her eyes betrayed her soul; you could see the evil in them. There was no warmth to this young woman. Even when her lips were smiling, you felt a chill when you looked at her icy, cold eyes.

She heard all the rumors about her father, Tyler, a shrewd businessman who had shattered many lives in his quest for more power and money. It didn't matter who he hurt, even friends of our family were destroyed by his ruthlessness.

She thought about Mathlide, her mother, who everyone called Mattie, she was a well-bred wealthy young woman, who found it impossible to cope with the contempt of her peers over her husband's unscrupulous dealings. She started losing her mind and was convinced that her husband personified a poisonous tree that could only bear evil fruit and Mala smiled, and thought yes indeed I'm a chip off the old block.

Mala gave her makeup its finishing touches by brushing just a touch of blush to her cheeks; I believe I took care of everything. I ordered three bottles of chilled champagne, a tray of assorted cheeses with imported crackers. For an assortment of appetizers I especially like the spareribs with the gingered plum sauce and the oyster's casino. That hotel staff better not screw up the fresh fruit I ordered dipped in chocolate or I will just have to get them all fired. Everything must be as I planned. He has to think that I am actually throwing a party for him and that insignificant redhead.

She put her hands on her hips as she gave herself one last glance in her full-length mirror. I look good, she thought, as she gathered up her small suitcase. I mustn't forget this, it cost me a pretty penny for the capsules and it just better work, or that old man who sold these to me will suffer big time!

She smiled as she left her apartment and thought of what was about to transpire. "Tonight, will be a night, I will never forget," she said out loud as she closed her apartment door. "I am about to have a very good time," as the sound of her laughter filled the empty hallway.

Spareribs and Gingered Plum Sauce

2 lbs of lean spareribs
5 tbsp. candied ginger chopped fine
1/3- cup soy sauce
5 tbsp. brown sugar
1 clove garlic, chopped fine
1 tbsp. cornstarch
1 cup pitted, mashed green plums
2 tbsp. vinegar

Simmer the spareribs in salted water until tender, about one hour and pull out all the bones. Cut the meat into strips about one inch long.

Mix the remaining ingredients, except the plums, and two tablespoons of the ginger. Thoroughly coat the meat with the mixture.

Arrange on a roasting pan and set the pan on the middle shelf of the broiler. Turn the broiler to high, leave the door open and watch carefully. When the tops are brown, turn the meat, brush with sauce and brown them. Remove from the broiler and drain the meat on absorbent paper. Mix the plums and remaining ginger and refrigerate both for twenty-four hours.

When ready to serve the meat, spear each piece on a pick. Place the gingered plum sauce in a small bowl and surround with the meat. Makes 10 to 15 appetizers

Oysters Casino

3 dozen freshly opened oysters
3 slices of bacon
½ cup minced green onions
¼ cup minced green pepper
¼ cup minced celery
1 tsp. Worcestershire sauce
2 drops Tabasco sauce

Preheat oven to hot (400 degrees F.) Place two drained oysters on the deep half on one shell. Arrange filled oysters shells on a layer of rock salt in one large baking pan or six individual shallow casseroles.

In a skillet cook the bacon until crisp; remove from the pan, drain. Season with lemon juice. Worcestershire sauce, and Tabasco.

Spoon the mixture on the oysters in the shells and top with the crumbled bacon. Bake ten minutes. Serves 6

The Crash

The last two years were the happiest in Janelle's life. She entered college early, at seventeen and a half studied hard and received a scholarship. She took on a full load of classes and loved every minute of it, especially English literature. She was always happiest with her books.

Beau had just graduated and in three days would be leaving for his home in Louisiana. Tonight, they were to make plans for her to visit him in New Orleans.

She still worked for Jake after school and made good money in tips. Mala and her friends constantly give her a hard time, but Beau made her feel that they were too insignificant to waste time thinking about them. She knew he was right; but every time Mala was around, Janelle felt a chill go up her spine. She tried not to think about her and focus on her date with Beau. In about three hours, she was to meet him at the Clover Inn, a popular bar and restaurant that was a hangout for all their friends.

She only worked the lunch shift at Jakes on Saturday and the rest of the day was hers. She took all her exams and was finished with school until the fall. She loved going to school. Sometime she would see or hear something and file it away in the back of her brain, ready to bring it out to use at a later time. Beau would laugh at her and say she suffered from sponge syndrome.

After work she ran home and as usual, her mom was in her darkened bedroom, and her dad was out. She knocked on her mom's door, and heard her tortured voice say, "Come in."

"Mom, I won't talk long, I just wanted to tell you I'm going out to meet Beau around eight or so. Would you like me to fix you some dinner?"

"No Janelle thanks." Beatrice tries to raise her head slowly, but the pain was too great.

Janelle poured her a glass of water, as Beatrice reached for her medication. After so many years of her mom's illness, Janelle knew exactly what to do. "Your father and I are going out to dinner tonight, I just took a pill and I'm sure I'll be feeling better shortly. You have fun; I'll see you when you come home."

"You and dad are going out? That's wonderful! Gosh, the two of you have not gone out together in years. I can't wait to hear all about it tomorrow morning," she said as she bent over and kissed her Moms forehead. Janelle gave her a hug and ran up to her room to get dressed for her date.

Janelle wanted to look nice tonight. Beau was leaving soon and she cherished their time together. She would never forget the past two years; they had been perfect. Since beau entered her life she had felt different, he made her feel pretty and desirable for the first time in her life. I guess that old saying was true, "A woman only feels pretty when she is loved." She would miss Beau when he left for New Orleans. That's why tonight was so important; they were to talk about their future together.

Let's see, she thought, what shall I wear? This navy vest and short skirt, or the blue blouse and slacks; she asked the mirror. No, this is it, as she held the dark green silk dress that Mary had made for her. It's just right with my red hair. She showered and dressed as quick as possible. The silk felt good against her skin, it made her feel desirable. Beau always said he liked the feel of silk. Hmm, Beau, just his names made her feel shaky, and when he held her in his arms, she felt like this must be heaven. She really was quite in love with him, and would be crushed if anything were to happen to their relationship.

As she left the house, she felt so light hearted that she did something she never remembered doing in her entire life. Her father was in the kitchen waiting for her mom to finish dressing for dinner. He looked great in his gray suit; it went well with his white hair. He had stopped drinking for at least four months, and she was just thrilled to see him sober.

"Wait right here," she said, as her mother entered the room looking so pretty. "I want to get my camera. The two of you just look so good I've got to take a picture."

She ran upstairs to her room, grabbed her camera and took a picture of her parents all dressed up and smiling. She gave them each a kiss, as she waved good-bye, and ran out the front door.

When Janelle entered the Inn she walked to the peach damask sofa by the fireplace, where she was to meet Beau at eight o'clock. She glanced at her watch and noted it was half past eight. It was unusual for Beau to be late.

The Inn was beautiful, with its dark wood floors and pastel print drapes. She especially liked the huge floral arrangements that sat on the antique bureau and tables. How clever, she thought, of the decorator to pick out all the colors in the drapes and follow through with the flowers and furniture. There was a comfortable pleasantness to it all.

She was noticing the smallest details that made up the

room, like the attractive small dishes filled with dried flowers, when she looked up and saw one of Mala's friends walking towards her. Janelle never really liked her; she always thought she was rather trampish in spite of all her family's wealth.

"If you're looking for Beau, he's in Room 204," she said with delight.

Janelle smiled and thanked her, as she picked up her purse to go meet Beau. She thought this was odd but maybe he was planning a private dinner party just for the two of them.

With anticipation, she walked up the stairs to the second floor and down the hallway into Room 204. As she knocked on the door, it swung open and there were Mala and Beau naked in bed. Janelle cried out, as Mala looked straight at her with a cold smile on her face. At that moment Janelle thought she could actually hear her heart breaking. She closed the door and ran out of the Inn, silently sobbing.

As she ran, Sandra was laughing and called out to her, "Janelle, leaving so soon? Did you congratulate Beau on his engagement to Mala?"

Feeling like her world had ended, not wanting to go home to an empty house, she walked over to Jake's place and just about fell into the booth. Sally looked up and immediately could tell by the stricken look on her friend's face that something was terribly wrong.

"What is it, honey? What has happened?"

Janelle couldn't talk, she was crying so hard. Her thin body was shaking with her sobs while Sally tried to console her, with a warm embrace.

"Now drink this water, it will calm you down. Ata girl, do you feel well enough to talk now? Come on child, it can't be that bad, can it?"

Janelle through tears streaming uncontrollably down her face blurted out everything that had happened. All the while, Sally is hugging her and saying over and over, "Hush now child, I know it hurts, but that's love. It always feels so good or so awful, there never seems to be an in-between stage."

As Janelle was sobbing her heart out, Joe and Leroy, two policemen friends of theirs entered the diner. Looking very troubled, they hesitantly walked up to Janelle. While Leroy took her hand, Joe stood there with his head down studying his shoes, as if they were very interesting, and about to do something too clever to miss.

Leroy cleared his throat, and looking so miserable said, "I would rather cut my heart out then tell you this Janelle. There has been a terrible accident out on Long Road," his voice cracked, as he wiped away a tear. No matter how often he was the bearer of bad news, it seemed to always affect him emotionally. There was no way to soften those terrible words. "I'm afraid your parents are both dead."

This was just too much pain for one person to bear in one night. Thankfully she collapsed into unconsciousness, with Sally holding her tight and sobbing. Even hard-nosed Jake was wiping the tears from his eyes.

Janelle's smile touched many people who were all very fond of her. Those who were close to her hated to see so much pain enter into her young life. This was the night her heart almost died.

That Awful Night

My head, it aches so. Why do I feel like I'm in some kind of fog? Oh God, I think my head is going to explode! Where the heck am I? As Beau opened his eyes and tried to focus, he cautiously looked around. The first rays of dawn were streaming into the room, like a beacon shinning directly on the spotted, light blue carpet. He looked at the ceiling, than ever so slowly, in spite of the pain; he turned his head to observe his surroundings.

He saw the roses on the wallpaper, the overstuffed blue velvet chair and the flowers on the bureau that were drooping and starting to turn brown around the edges. Why is nothing familiar?

He tried to sit up, but his head was throbbing so much, he had to lay back and close his eyes until the pain subsided. Suddenly, he was aware that he was not alone; there was movement next to him. Confused and afraid of what he might find he reluctantly turned to see Mala naked and asleep. Shocked at the sight of Mala, he sat up abruptly, and almost cried out in pain as he reaches for his shirt.

Oh no, not Mala! I would have chosen anyone but Mala. How did I get myself in this mess? Even though his head was throbbing and he had a terrible taste in his mouth, he started to get dressed as fast as he could.

He almost passed out as he bent over to tie his shoes, the pain in his eyes was excruciating. He tried to focus, to remember how he got into this mess. He rubbed his eyes, and then massaged his temples to relax. It all started to come back to him. When he had arrived at the inn, he was given a message from Janelle to meet him in room 204. He thought, how nice, she probably had arranged a private dinner just for the two of them.

He had gone up to the room, knocked on the door and was very surprised when Mala opened the door. She had a very nice table in the center of the room filled with various appetizers, and fresh fruit, dipped in chocolate. There was a bottle of his favorite wine on the table and several glasses. It looked like it was set up for a small party.

"Surprise!" said Mala. "I know I haven't been the nicest person in the world toward you and Janelle, and I just wanted to make amends. So, I planned this little party to tell you how sorry I am for being so awful."

"It's very sweet of you Mala, to go through all this trouble just for me and Janelle. I really am touched."

"Come," she said as she took his hand, "have some wine while we wait for the others to show up." She poured wine for the two of them, and said, "For old time's sake, Beau, and for what could have been."

Those were the last words he heard. He shook his head, and winced from the pain, what a fool I was, he thought. I should have known better, a leopard never changes his spots; and Mala was never sorry for anything she did. He knew now he had been drugged. That explained the throbbing head and the unusual taste in his mouth.

Mala stretched, like a satisfied cat, and turned over in the bed as she started to slowly wake up. She reached over to touch Beau, but he was already up and almost dressed.

"Your' awake?" she asked rather puzzled. "They said

you wouldn't be able to stand or function for days." She frowned as she tried to sort these new events out in her head. "Huh? Let me fix you another drink!"

He didn't answer, just frowned and finished dressing.

"Where are you going?" she smiled, still at ease with herself and the situation. "We've been having such a good time. I thought maybe we could have a repeat performance this morning."

When Beau finally turned to look at her, she saw the look of anger on his face, and she knew she had gone much too far. Up to now he had always been polite to her, but now all she saw was pure rage and hatred.

The way he looked at her startled her; she just couldn't understand what he was so upset about. "You know," Mala said with as much conviction as possible, "Making love to me was all your idea. What are you so upset about? We did have fun, the last few nights, didn't we?"

Few nights! Oh God no, he thought, as he continued to dress as quickly as possible.

Mala jumped out of bed and brazenly walks over to him stark naked. She tried to put her arms around his neck, but he savagely pushed her away.

"Look at me! Don't you think I'm perfect?' She stepped back so he could see her full firm breasts and her flat stomach.

His reply was in a very even toneless voice, filled with such loathing, the likes of which she had never heard in her life. "I think you are the vilest creature I have ever had the misfortune to know. I hope I never have to lay eyes on you again, naked or fully dressed, as long as I live." He reached for the door, and was about to leave when he heard Mala's words cut through the air like flying daggers.

"Oh, do you still think your precious Janelle will still want you after she saw you with me the other night?"

He slowly turned around with a very quizzical look on his face. "You arranged all this so that Janelle and I would break up? How could you be so self-centered and contempt-ible? Did you really think that drugging me would ever bring me closer to you? I don't think so, not now or ever! I would never consider getting intimate with someone as low class as you."

As he turned to leave, Mala lost all control. How dare anyone put her down? She started smashing everything in sight; he could hear her fury as he walked down the hallway and into the elevator. If they should meet at one of the many functions in New Orleans, he wondered how he could ever be civil to her again.

He felt like he needed to go to his apartment and take a hot shower, but that had to wait. He went to the nearest phone and called his friend Gus.

"Acme Laboratory," said the perky voice.

"Could you please connect me to Gus Tuston?"

"Yes sir."

The sound of the phone ringing made Beau very ner-vous. What if he's not there? What will I do? He felt his body stop trembling when after four rings he heard his friend's voice.

"This is Gus Tuston, can I help you?"

"Thank God your there man, I need you help."

"Beau, buddy what's up?"

"I need a blood test right away. I believe I have ingested a drug. I want to know what kind it is, and I want it doc-umented. Could you fit me in right now? I'm not far, only about twenty minutes away.

"Sure Beau, come right over, don't drink or eat anything until you've been tested, OK?"

"Thanks Gus, I'm on my way." Beau hung up the phone

overwhelmed with relief that Gus was there for him. I'll take care of the test first, and maybe Gus could give me something for this awful headache. Then, I will find Janelle, he thought, I just have to tell her what happened and hope she understands.

When Beau returned from the test he headed straight for the shower. He has been scrubbing his skin for the last forty-five minutes, but he just couldn't work up enough lather from the soap to satisfy him. No matter how often he would scrub his body and then rinse off, he still felt dirty. He was trying so hard to scrub away Mala's scent, but it wouldn't go away. Since he regained consciousness, and found himself in bed with her, he realized what she had done to him.

Straight from the Inn he had gone to see his friend Gus, who worked at Acme Laboratory. He told him what had happened, and he wanted to know what Mala had given him. Gus took a blood sample, and handed Beau a specimen cup. "Here," he said, "You know what to do with it." Gus promised Beau he would work on the blood and urine samples immediately and probably would have an answer for him in an hour.

Beau tried calling Janelle from the lab but there wasn't any answer, which seemed king of strange since her mom was always home. What must Janelle be thinking? Everything happened so fast. One moment he was to meet her at the Inn for dinner and drinks and the next moment, he realized that three days have disappeared from his life. Where was she? He loved her so much, he was going to propose to her the night he was to meet her at the Inn. Whenever he thought of her he grew weak with desire.

He rinsed himself off again, turned off the shower and heard the phone ringing. Maybe it was Janelle. He grabbed a towel and ran for the phone while trying to dry him -self off. He picked up the phone and said, "Hello," hoping again that it was Janelle.

"Hey buddy, it's Gus, got your results back and they are unbelievable! You must be living a very charmed life. Not only are you good looking and rich but you are the luckiest guy I know."

"Why?"

"Well let me ask you what did you do and more importantly, what did you drink before you went to the Inn?"

Beau thought for a minute, it seemed so long ago, and then said, "Oh yeah, I had gone for a run and when I got back I was so thirsty I drank the only thing I had in the fridge; half a gallon of cranberry juice. I just about drank the whole bottle."

"Now that's why you were so lucky. You were slipped a drug that was in the wine called GHB an easily manufactured colorless and odorless liquid. This knockout drug is classified as a sedative hypnotic. It can cause memory loss, unconsciousness, coma or even seizures."

"This is a good thing? That's why I'm so lucky?"

"No," Gus laughed, it's because you drank a lot of cranberry juice. You see most times you would have woken up, if you woke up at all, and not remembered a thing. Complete loss of memory, like who you had a drink with, or how you got there, or what had happened. The cranberry juice offset the potency of the drug. My mother always told me cranberry juice was good for you, and I'll bet even she didn't know just how good."

Beau sighed, he tried to quell the feeling in the pit of his stomach, this time Mala went much too far! What was she thinking? He shook his head when he thought about how close he came to slipping into a coma. "Gus, I just can't thank you enough. Could you mail the results to my New

Orleans address? So much has happened to me the last three days and now this afternoon is my flight back home. I can't change it because my family is planning a party for me and over two hundred people will be there. I have to get dressed, pack and see if I could find Janelle. I want to ask her something before I leave."

"Good luck to you Beau. I'll mail you the report and hopefully we'll get together soon. Oh and by the way," Gus laughed before he hung up, "watch what you drink."

Beau was still holding the phone to his ear, listening to the dial tone and thinking about how low Mala had sunk. But like a little voice going off in the back of his brain, he thought, wasn't there some scandal about her mother?

He dialed Janelle's number again, but it just rang and rang over and over again. He hung up, and was about to dial Jake's place when he glanced at his watch and realized he barely had time to make his flight. He dressed very quickly, packed his clothes, threw three days of mail into his gym bag, and left for the airport.

Once on the plane Beau read his mail and smiled as he discovered a letter from Janelle. All of a sudden his hands shook as he opened the letter and his smiled turned to a frown as he read Janelle's letter congratulating him on his engagement to Mala. His heart dropped down to his stomach. He was stunned. What was she told? He had to speak with her and now.

Beau reached for the phone that was attached to the back of the seat in front of him, punched in the credit card number and dialed her home number again. Once more there was no answer. He then dialed the number of Jake's Place and on the fourth ring Sally answered saying, "Jake's Place, Sally speaking. How can I help you?"

"Sally, it's me, Beau. Is Janelle there? I've been calling

her house and there is no answer, is she there?" This was the only time that Beau could remember when Sally was silent. She didn't utter a sound. He then says, "I got this crazy letter from her congratulating me on my engagement, and with all people Mala. What's this all about?"

Finally Sally spoke, "Don't you know Beau?"

"Sally right now I'm on a flight to New Orleans and 10,000 feet in the air. Would I be calling you if I knew?"

"Oh Beau don't you know that Janelle saw you and Mala together in bed making love, and don't you know that both of Janelle's parents died in an automobile accident that very same night? She was so pitiful, so very hurt by everything that after the funeral Mary and I sent her to Europe to heal. We couldn't think of anything else to do. We know she used to read all those books about traveling to different lands, so we thought a change of scenery would be good for her."

Beau listened to Sally's voice, not quite understanding of what he was hearing.

"She had us so worried. She was so alone and close to a mental breakdown. Beau, how could you have done that to her? We're talking about Janelle, a person so sweet she couldn't even step on a bug. She is the kindest gentlest person I've ever known. In one night she lost everything that was dear to her. You almost destroyed her Beau. Shame on you," she said as she hung up the phone.

Beau once again was staring into space listening to a dial tone. The flight attendant asked him to please replace the phone on the cradle because they were on the final approach into New Orleans.

His world had collapsed. The one person, that he loved, more than life itself had needed him and he had not been there for her. Both of her parents were gone in one terrible night. What she must have gone through. Damn that Mala.

I'll never forgive her he thought as wiped his eyes that started to cloud up.

He looked out the window of the aircraft at the bright blue sky, with the puffy white clouds and it all looked so peaceful. Somewhere out there under this same sky was Janelle and at that moment he felt so close to her. How he wished he could reach out and touch her hand. He put his head down and with eyes closed silently prayed as he whispered, "Oh God please help me find her."

The plane slowly descended into the New Orleans airport, and just as the wheels touched the runway, Beau's body shook with a hushed sob, that he tried so hard to hold back.

Soon he would be wrapped in the warmth of his family. They were thrilled that he had graduated with honors and had made the dean's list. In just a few hours he must smile and pretend that he was happy; while all the time he felt like he just got punched in the stomach and couldn't breathe.

Mala will probably be at the party with her father; it was going to be very hard to be in the same room with her. He knew how powerful and ruthless her father was. He was well known for destroying quite a few lives to get what he wanted, including his wife's. Beau wished his father didn't have to do business with someone so merciless. He tapped his fingers rapidly on the arm of the seat, a nervous habit that Janelle used to tease him about. "Janelle," he murmured, "how will I ever make this up to you?"

His mind was speeding with ways to contact her. He would have to give her time. He knew someday he would make it up to her. He just had to think of a way, because he knew…he could never live in this world without her.

Time to Heal

If it weren't for the moisture collecting on her jacket, she could hardly tell it was raining. Riding down the Rhine in the calm of the early morning hours was turning out to be one of her very favorite things to do in this new land she was visiting. The combination of early dawn and the pulsing of the boat on the calm water made her feel so tranquil. She was almost able to forget the anguish that caused her to leave Crestview, California.

Finally she was doing what she always dreamed of as a child; she was traveling through Europe. Janelle should be thrilled. This was exactly what she always wanted to do, but she felt so heartsick. She would have given up all her dreams, if only she could see her parents just one more time.

She was amazed when after the funeral of her parents; an insurance agent approached her and handed her a check for four hundred thousand dollars. It seems her father had insurance policies on both her mom and himself with a face value of one hundred thousand dollars each. The policies included double indemnity clauses in the event of accidental deaths. It was so ironic that after all the years her father had driven drunk, now that he was sober, he should be killed by a drunk driver.

Janelle would have gone completely out of her mind, if

it were not for her friends Mary and Sally. They not only took care of her, but also made all the arrangements for the funeral and put the furniture in storage. They suggested she get away for a while and bought her a ticket for a tour of Europe. Both Sally and Mary wanted to go with her, but she assured them that she had to be alone for a few months, so she could think about everything and take this time to heal.

So many questions were going around in her head. Why had Beau tricked her? He made her feel like he was really interested in her, when all along, it was Mala. Did he feel like she wouldn't fit into his life style? Perhaps it was because of her back ground, yes that must be it, he felt she couldn't adapt to his way of life.

She wondered if he and Mala often got together after he, walked her home. Was this feeling of love she thought he also felt only a dream? Why didn't he tell her he cared for Mala? Why the deception? Why did he ever enter into her life; and how…was she ever going to live without him?

She made Mary and Sally promise to give the letter she had written to Beau, congratulating him on his engagement and hoping his future would be bright with Mala by his side. She was so deep in thought that she hadn't noticed that someone was standing beside her.

"It's rather brisk this morning," said the very attractive elderly woman. "Aren't you cold my dear with just that little jacket on?"

"What you need is a wool scarf, like we have," said her husband.

"Well don't just talk about it Percy, go get her one! Bring her the blue cashmere; it would look wonderful with her bright red hair. My name my dear, is Elizabeth Graves, but please just call me Lizzie. Elizabeth is just too long and formal."

"It's so nice to meet you." Janelle said as they shook hands. "My name is Janelle Connors from Crestview, California." She immediately took a liking to both of them. Perhaps it was the twinkle in Lizzie's faded blue eyes whenever she spoke. Or could it be that she was starting to feel very lonely, and just welcomed their companionship?

"Here you are my dear," said Percy as he draped the wool scarf over Janelle's shoulders. She shuddered ever so slightly with the warmth of the scarf as the chill she had felt left her body. "I must say this is beautiful country. I'm sure you don't want to miss one of the most scenic parts of the valley by going inside, I know, Lizzie perhaps we should order a pot of hot tea while we show our new friend the huge rocks with the water cascading over them. If memory serves me right, they should be just around the bend."

"Sounds wonderful Percy, and order some of those wonderful scones. You will join us, won't you Janelle?"

"Yes of course, I'd be delighted."

Drinking tea in the company of this delightful English couple, made the ride on the Rhine from Switzerland to Germany through the Black Forest and into France, a very enjoyable event. They were very informative about how the upper Rhine is fed by the melting snow of the Alps. The water is usually very high in the late spring or summer here at the alpine section of Basel. The beech and oak trees along the shoreline were beautiful, so different from the palm trees along the shores of Lake Lucano. Every now and then she would see an eagle, with its magnificent wings spread out, flying high in the sky, or a wild boar running through the forest in search of its prey. The ride on the Rhine was actually very therapeutic.

While sipping hot tea, they pointed to the valley walls beneath the ruined castles, which were terraced for growing grapes to make wine. Janelle could not understand how they could harvest the grapes on such steep slopes. The Germans were ingenious; to cultivate every piece of land in their domain, nothing was wasted.

The Graves told her they had made this trip once a year for the past twelve years in honor of their only son. He had been killed in a mountain climbing accident in the Alps. The trip somehow brought them closer to him, if only in their memories.

Janelle told them about Mary, Sally and Jake, her friends, or should she say her family, and how they had arranged this trip for her. She had flown from Los Angeles to Lucerne, Switzerland. She really enjoyed this part of the world, especially the cooking classes she had been taking for the last two weeks. She described to Lizzie the marvelous pastries she had learned to bake. Bondepige Med Slor was her favorite.

Lizzie was nodding her head as she exclaimed, "I know that cake, Percy and I had it for dessert just last week. It's wonderful, but just a bit rich for me."

Janelle smiled at Lizzie and Percy and told them of the trip into the mountains she and her fellow students had taken. How she came upon this great artists' colony, tucked away near one of the most popular ski chalets. She told them of the beautiful painting she bought of the very old chalet surrounded by mountains and exquisite pine trees. Joseph, a local artist with huge hands signed the painting and had invited her and her friends to a party. Now every time she looks at the picture she will remember the marvelous time she had and the interesting people she has met and how they all promised to keep in touch.

"Percy and I know of that ski chalet, if memory serves me right, let's see, I believe it was one day after a heavy snowfall, we had been skiing for hours and were frozen and exhausted. Quite by chance, we came upon this fantastic lodge in the middle of nowhere. What a wonderful feeling it was to find this lovely haven, with its rich wood paneling and blazing fireplaces. Is that the same lodge?"

"Yes that's the one."

"Do you by any chance remember that fabulous Goulash Soup they made?"

"I loved it, said Janelle. I enjoyed it so much that I just had to have the recipe. After dinner, I asked to see the chef so I could compliment him. He was a very tall, heavyset man with this thick Hungarian accent and a mustache that went on forever. He was quite a character with the most amusing stories. I promised I would write to him when I made the goulash."

"Percy and I thought we were in heaven when we were consuming that meal, while sitting by the fireplace, so nice and warm. It was wonderful to feel so cozy while looking out the windows at the terrible blizzard outside. Of course the Austrian beer, with which we were washing down the Goulash only added to our joy. Now that was a good time. You remember don't you Percy?"

He looked at her and smiled, "Yes my love, I do remember every minute of that wonderful day and night," as he took her hand and kissed it.

Lizzie noticed the look of sadness that came across Janelle's face. She reminded Lizzie of a wounded bird whose wings had been clipped and found it impossible to fly. Her heart went out to this troubled pretty young girl.

Janelle found the Graves very easy to talk to and by the time the ship had reached the Black Forest they were all good friends. One night over a glass of wine, Janelle for the very first time since the accident, told then about how heartsick she was over the death of her parents.

Perhaps because both she and the Graves had shared terrible losses, there was an immediate bond between them. Lizzie looked at Percy and he nodded approval. It was uncanny but true that with some couples who are very close to each other, know instinctively what is on the other person's mind without uttering a word.

"My dear," said Lizzie, "It's impossible to appreciate this beautiful continent in only a few months. We have a suggestion for you that perhaps you would like to consider. We have a very large flat in London overlooking Regent's Park. Do you know the history of the park?"

"No," said Janelle, "but I'd like to know about it."

"Well it's rather an interesting tale about Royalty. King Henry the eighth bought this parcel of land for hunting purposes only. He made sure the deer remained in the confines of the park and the poachers outside of it. The one sport his majesty loved was hunting. He would invite several kings and princes from other kingdoms to come hunting with him, right up until the day he died.

"That is an interesting tale."

"In time the elite hired Nash, a most famous architect of the times to build magnificent homes with long terraces overlooking the peacefulness of the park. Unfortunately most of the buildings were partially destroyed during the bombings of World War two."

"How sad, it sounds like it was a lovely place to live."

"Well, Percy and I thought that too. So when the war ended, we bought one of the bombed out houses. Luckily it was summer, and we were able to live in the house while it was being renovated. The roof was mostly gone and the pipes were destroyed so there wasn't any running water."

"How did you do it? Where did you cook, or take a bath?"

"It was very frustrating at first," said Lizzie as her brow furrowed and she began to remember that awful time, "but we quickly mastered all the necessary lessons of survival. I learned how to cook over an open fire in our fireplace. We would bathe in Regent's Park's lake, and took care of our bodily functions with a portable privy."

"I can't begin to imagine what it must have been like, to live every day without all the conveniences that we take so much for granted, like electricity and running water."

"I must admit," said Lizzie as she sighed, "the war showed me the worst and the best side of humanity. It was a period of learning. Oh, not only about the renovation but also about what is important in one's life. You see Janelle; I have lived long enough to know that life is a journey. Each step along the way is a time for learning, for without experiencing the good as well as the bad, it would be a very empty existence. The beauty of life depends in how you choose to live it, and believe me, you do have a choice."

"Yes, I understand, but Lizzie how do you get over the hurt."

"Oh, that's easy, you don't wait. You simply get on with your life. Eventually the pain becomes only a memory."

"I see, of course your right. It does seem that with the passing of each day, the hurt lessens."

Taking Janelle's hand, Lizzie says, "Trust me child, your heart will heal, it just takes time."

Janelle wiped away a tear, smiled and said, "Now tell me how, did you manage to restore your home."

"Well, supplies were almost impossible to come by, especially things like metal pipes and electrical wires. There wasn't any iron at all, even the wrought iron railings were pulled out of the homes, so that they could be melted down and made into tanks. We had to literally sift through demolished building for used plumbing pipes, moldings, and electrical parts, anything else that could be salvaged.

"You strike me as such a gentile lady it is difficult for me to picture you dirty and scrounging through the rubble of a destroyed building."

Lizzie just laughed as she said, "Well, I did it because I had to. Sometimes when life deals you a blow, you discover an inner strength that you never dreamed you had. It's there in everyone you just have to look for it."

"I know," said Janelle. "I believe I am learning, thanks to you."

"I hope my story helps. As we progressed, we added some of the modern conveniences, such as central heat and air conditioning. Even though it was a very difficult time for us, trying to restore the house to its original charm, it also was a time of joy."

"Most definitely!" said Percy. "You know, Janelle, the flat has three levels. We reside on the first and second floors. The third one has three furnished rooms, a bath, and a very lovely terrace that overlooks the park. Why don't you come live with us and finish your last year of college in London? On holidays, we could take the train or fly to Italy, France, or Spain. This way you could really see the world. Why we could even introduce you to the Queen."

"You know the Queen?" exclaimed Janelle with wide eyes.

"Oh yes, for years, we've been invited to their doings," said Percy. "Sometimes the parties are stimulating and other times downright dull," he added.

"Not only that," chimed in Lizzie, "but if you're fond of cooking classes, I'm sure we could arrange for you to learn from the most famous chefs in London. The General Manager of The Savoy is a personal friend of ours for many years and I know he could arrange it. These chefs were trained in kitchens by others who learned their craft from the greatest chef of all Auguste Escoffier."

"Escoffier, but he was famous! Didn't he work at the Grand Hotel in Monte Carlo? Oh, and come to think of it, wasn't he responsible for introducing French cuisine at the Ritz Hotels in New York City?"

"Yes, it's a known fact that he trained generations of talented chefs in the finest hotels in the world. Why I do believe that it was he who was responsible for establishing French cooking as the standard for western cuisine. You really know your chefs for a young American girl."

Janelle just laughed and said, "Lizzie, I would really love to come and share the flat with you and Percy. I believe I do need a change and I think this will be the start of a new beginning and a wonderful friendship."

She was right. It really was the start of a new life. Janelle could not face being alone just yet, and thought she needed a change away from Crestview and the memories of her mother and father. Away from the vision she could not erase of Beau and Mala together. Away from the memory of that awful night when her world had ended and she had collapsed. This change would be good for her; it was time to heal, to get on with her life, to start…the journey.

Bondepige Med Slør

8 tbsp. unsalted butter
3 tbsp. sugar
1 tbsp butter softened
2 tbsp. grated semisweet baking chocolate
3 cups fine, dry bread crumbs made from dark rye or
    pumpernickel bread
2-$\frac{1}{2}$ cups applesauce, canned or homemade
2 tbsp. unsalted butter, cut into $\frac{1}{2}$ inch bits
1 cup chilled heavy cream
2 to 3 tbsp. raspberry jam

In a heavy 1-iinch skillet, melt the 8 tablespoons of butter over moderate heat. When the foam subsides, add the bread-crumbs and sugar. Stir with a wooden spoon. Turn down the heat to low and continue stirring until the mixture is evenly browned and the breadcrumbs are dry and crisp. Remove from the heat stir in the grated chocolate and mix until thoroughly melted. Set the pan aside to cool a little.

Preheat the oven to 375o. Lightly grease a shallow 1 quart mold, soufflé' dish or cake pan with the 1 tablespoon of soft butter, and cover the bottom of the dish with a $\frac{1}{2}$ inch layer of the browned crumbs. Spoon on a thick layer of the applesauce, and then another of bread crumbs, alter-nating until all the ingredients have been used. Top with a layer of crumbs and dot with the 2- tablespoon of butter cut into $\frac{1}{4}$ inch bits. Bake for 25 minutes in the center of the oven and let the cake cool.

Before serving, beat the chilled heavy cream in a large chilled mixing bowl with a wire whisk, hand or electric beater until it just holds its shape. Use the whipped cream to top the cake, and decorate, if desired, with dabs of the raspberry jam.

Goulash Soup

2 tbsp. oil for sautéing
3 medium onions, peeled and diced
2 tbsp. tomato puree
$\frac{1}{4}$ cup flour
1 tbsp. sweet Hungarian paprika
1 tbsp. red wine vinegar
6 cups bouillon
8 oz. Lean beef, cut into 1-inch cubes
1 garlic clove, peeled and crushed
$\frac{1}{2}$ tsp. caraway seeds
$\frac{1}{2}$ tsp. dried marjoram
salt to taste
3 medium potatoes, peeled and cut into $\frac{1}{2}$ inch cubes

Traditionally thought of as a Hungarian dish, goulash is a part of Austrian cuisine.

1. Heat the oil in a skillet and sauté the onions until they are golden brown. Add the tomato puree and remove from the heat.
2. Stir in the flour and then the paprika. Add the vinegar and then the bouillon. Stir well and return to the heat.
3. Bring to a boil and add the meat, garlic, caraway, marjoram, and salt to taste. Allow to boil, uncovered, until the meat is tender.
4. Add the potatoes and continue boiling, uncovered, until they are tender but firm.
5. The goulash should be served while piping hot.

The Journey Begins

It didn't take long to become acclimated to her new sur-roundings; the small apartment was just perfect. The bed-room had a light mauve silk chaise lounge or as it used to be called, a fainting sofa. There was a dresser with a huge mirror, an armoire, and in the middle of the room stood a four- poster dark mahogany bed with a white lacy canopy and bed skirt. The antique hand quilted white, mauve and green bedspread conjured a feeling of coziness, and warmth.

A second room was simply furnished with a desk, a chair, a small colorfully printed sofa with a matching up-holstered chair, and a beautiful fireplace that made the room warm and comfortable.

The small fireplace had a cream colored marble mantle, where Janelle had placed a picture of her mom and dad, the one that was taken in the kitchen the last time she saw them alive. There was also a photo of a smiling Janelle when she was ten wearing an apron that Mary had crocheted for her. The two of them were standing by the stove stirring the sauce. She missed her parents terribly and she missed the good times she had cooking with Mary.

Of course, she had to have a picture of Sally with her arms full of dinner plates and a big smile on her face. A person just had to feel good whenever they thought about Sally. She was always so much fun to be around.

The last picture on the mantle was a small snapshot of Janelle sitting with a lap full of books while being embraced from behind by a smiling Beau. She wondered if she would ever stop longing for him.

In the tiny den of the small apartment, was a floor to ceiling library. The bronze floor lamp gave off a soft glow on the dark green velvet upholstered chair and matching ottoman, where Janelle spent many peaceful hours doing what she liked best...reading books.

The window in her sitting room had long rose-colored velvet drapes bunched up at the floor to prevent drafts. When the drapes were left open the window gave off a marvelous view of Regents Park. She would walk out onto her terrace on a sunny day with a cup of tea observing her surroundings. She was never bored watching the activities of the joggers and cyclist, running and walking through the park.

Regents Park had magnificently tall iron gates that reflected an elegance of a bygone era. Sometimes she would walk by the beautiful flowerbeds or sit under the shade of the trees, listening to the sound of the flowing water from the Triton Fountains.

On Sundays, she would pack a few books in a tote bag and walk to the bridge that overlooked the canal. There were always boatloads of people riding up and down the waterway. Janelle would sit under the oak tree and listen to the band playing lovely waltzes and old Cole Porter tunes. It all had a civilized quietness about it. The ambiance of the park filled her soul with peace.

It was a breathtaking view of life in London. But at times, she would look at the couples holding hands and kissing, remembering all the times she and Beau had spent by the ocean and her heart would ache.

Slowly Janelle was healing. Each day while staying with the Graves was filled with an adventure. True to their word she did meet the Queen along with dignitaries from all over the world. The exciting life she had always dreamed of was now a reality.

So many interesting people were starting to fill her life with joy, especially Lizzie's next door neighbors, the Tans. Being Chinese fugitives from Beijing, their stories were always stimulating. It was right after the incident in Tieneman square that they were forced to leave their country with just the clothes on their backs, while running for their lives.

However before leaving their beloved land, they retrieved hidden jewels that had been given to their great uncle twenty years ago, by the child emperor for performing a courageous deed. This fortune in diamonds was sewn into the shoulder pads of their coats. Janelle spent many nights listening to their fascinating stories of life under the communist rule, while playing Mah Jong, and ancient game from the Ming Dynasty. She would be equally mesmerized by both the enticing stories and the hypnotic game.

Percy and Lizzie opened a whole new world to her. A world of knowledge, about a land and its history and she was fascinated by it all.

She enjoyed her classes at Cambridge and met an interesting group of students who took her to all the favorite haunts of the literary groups. She sat in pubs where Noel Coward had frequented and went to the Savoy Theater where Gilbert and Sullivan's first musical plays were performed.

Once she was invited to a country house that had entertained F Scott Fitzgerald and his tortured wife Zelda. As she sat in the living room and looked around she thought, of all the interesting, exciting people who once were in this very room. If only the walls could talk she wondered what stories they could tell.

The Graves introduced her to the Duke of Wellington, a young man that Janelle would always assimilate as the brother she never had. He brought her to several popular restaurants, where she was introduced to London's famous chefs.

Once, the Duke took her to the Shakespearean Theater to see the Taming of the Shrew. At the conclusion of the play, he and Janelle went backstage to meet the entire cast and wound up inviting everyone to his house for an impromptu party. It was fun to eat and drink with such talented people, discussing acting and the theater until dawn. Janelle had such a good time with them, that for a while, she was actually happy.

The Duke prided himself on his cooking skills. He taught Janelle how to make Beef Wellington, a recipe handed down to him form his ancestors. Together they would throw lavish parties for all of his and the Graves friends. The mix of young and old people was interesting and the conversations always enlightening. The Duke was fun to be with and his presence helped ease her pain.

Whenever she had a holiday from Cambridge, the Graves would take her to visit friends in other countries. Once they stayed in a villa in Madrid, which belonged to Senior Perez, owner of the largest art gallery in all of Spain.

Senior Perez was very knowledgeable in the arts. He showed her the architectural designs of Gaudi, and the artistic tapestries that filled his home. It was here that she learned about art and artists. Not only would he explain the painting, but also the emotional state of the artist at the time he had painted his masterpiece. He showed her the war scenes painted by Goya and explained how the onset of his deafness at the early of forty five made his work take on a more reflective character, especially in his portraits.

She studied the work of El Greco; Picasso and Salvador Dali's outrages paintings made her wonder what kind of mind would create such outlandish scenes.

Janelle purchased two paintings and an antique vase from Senor Perez, which she had shipped to Mary's home in Crestview. She smiled as she thought of Mary's attic bursting at the seams with all her newfound treasures.

As a souvenir of her stay in Spain, Senor Perez gave Janelle a print of a painting that Pablo Picaso had done during his blue period called Woman Ironing. She loved that painting and would treasure it always.

During summer vacation, Janelle took a cooking class in Rome at the Scaldaviande Cooking School, which in English means, "The Covered Dish."

The course was taught in English at a 17th century Roman Palazzo. It was all very interesting and informative and she came home with many wonderful recipes. One savory dish in particular was Saltimbocca, (little veal rolls), which she prepared for the Graves and the duke when she returned to England. They loved it so much they required she cook it every Sunday.

The Graves were wonderful people, surrounded by interesting friends, who gave her a peek at the good life and it really was a good life. Combinations of rich cultural history of the countries she visited, informative dinner conversations encompassing politics to environment, to developing third world countries, all contributed to make her an informed well-rounded individual.

She met a variety of people some rich some poor, some talented and others in a learning mode, so full of hope. All had one thing in common no matter what their circumstances they were seeking the same things, acceptance and love. Everyone needs to be loved and in this respect Janelle felt she was blessed. Lizzie was right it's a wonderful life, if you just know how to live it to its fullest.

However when alone, she felt like something was missing from her existence. She would have a sinking feeling in the pit of her stomach and invariably the tears would start. She was experiencing this uneasiness when she heard Percy calling her.

"I'm sitting out on the terrace with a pot of tea Percy. Come and join me," she said secretly grateful for the company as she dried her eyes.

He came out onto the terrace as she poured him a cup of tea. He pulled a chair up to the table, took a sip of tea, and a loud sigh escaped his lips, as he visibly collapsed.

"You're doing too much Percy you should learn how to rest a little more.'

"I know, I do feel a little worn out," he said as he reaches into his pocket." I picked this up from the postal box. It's a letter for you from the States."

She always felt good whenever she heard from her friends at home. Her face lit up as she opened the letter from Sally.

"Dear Janelle," she read, "hope this letter finds you well and happy. So much has happened in the two years you've been away. Mary and I miss you very much. Speaking of Mary, I have been arguing with her just about every day to go see Dr Melton. I just don't like the way she is coughing, but you know how stubborn she can be.

Jake sends his love. As usual he is working very hard at the diner, and of course, complains about it every day. You know him, Janelle, he keeps saying he wants to sell the diner and move to Florida where his sister lives. Now I know he's been saying this for years, but I really think this time he means it.

Oh yes, one more thing, I believe I met Mr. Right! I know you're probably saying again? But this time it's different. He's a retired educator and a world traveler. Could you imagine me with a smart man? I can't wait for you to meet him. Life is really just one big mystery.

Well I've got to go Janelle, please take care of yourself, and I miss you something terrible." Love Sally

Janelle's eyes were very misty as she finished reading the letter. Perhaps she should return home to Crestview. This letter had her worried about Mary and besides, she was feeling awfully homesick lately.

Percy was watching her read the letter, knowing as he observed her face, that she missed her home. "It's time, isn't it," he said.

"What do you mean Percy?"

"You know we are going to miss you very much if you should leave us. I really wish you would stay with Lizzie and me indefinitely, but I can see that it is time for you to get on with your own life."

"Oh, there you go again reading my thoughts. How do you do that?" she said smiling to cover her sadness. "The truth is I have been feeling a little homesick lately and I've been thinking about returning to the States."

"What are you two talking about?" asked Lizzie as she walked onto the terrace and poured herself a cup of tea.

"I think Janelle is going to be leaving us soon," said Percy with a lump in his throat. "She is returning to California."

"Oh Janelle, I'm going to miss you so much," said Lizzie with tears brimming in her eyes. "Why are you going back?"

"Well Lizzie, I think I'm going to be buying myself a restaurant, you know the diner that I always talked about. It seems the owner Jake is getting ready to retire and it really is a prime piece of real estate. I learned a lot about renovating from the two of you and would like to turn the diner into a posh restaurant."

"It sounds like a good idea, what with the cooking lessons you've taken from all the greatest chefs in Europe, I'm sure your restaurant will be a huge success. Now what can Percy and I do to help you? I know... we'll find antique dishes from every country and send them to you. This way you'll always be in our heart and thoughts."

Janelle hugged them both, and said through the tears streaming down her face, "I will definitely keep in touch with the two of you for the rest of my life. I don't know what I have done to deserve such good friends, but I know I'm very thankful to the heavens for sending you to me.

Percy stood and said, "Before you leave us, we are going to have a ball in your honor. We'll invite everyone that you have met throughout Europe."

"Right," said Lizzie as she stood up, "let's see, get some paper Percy, we have to make a list. This time we cannot forget to invite the Duke of Winchester and oh Percy, do you think the Queen could come?"

Janelle only smiled and thought, I really will miss them. I did have a great time and met wonderful people whom I will never forget. She lowered her head, massaged her forehead and whispered, "Now that I'm going home, maybe the nightmares will stop and I'll be able to sleep."

Saltimbocca

2 lbs. Of veal cutlets, sliced very thin
8 slices smoked ham (or prosciutto)
8 fresh sage leaves (or $\frac{1}{2}$ teaspoon dried sage)
$\frac{1}{4}$ cup of butter
Water or dry white wine

The preparation is simple. Cut the veal into 8 strips and pound them as thin as possible. Place a slice of ham, (cut to the same size of the veal), and place it on each strip with half a sage leaf between the two layers. Roll the saltimbocca, fasten with toothpicks, and brown in butter. Pour a little water or wine over it, cover and cook till tender. The juice should be thick, but scant. Before serving, pour juice over the veal rolls. Serve 6

Country Style Beef Wellington
(prepare a day ahead)

5 lbs center cut of filet beef roast

14 oz can mushrooms, drained and finely chopped

18 oz pkg. Liverwurst

1 tsp. salt

1 ½ tsp. of celery seeds

½ cup plus 2 tablespoons of cold water

½ cup finely chopped onion

2 tbs. melted butter

3 cups sifted flour

3 tbs. chopped parsley

2/3 cups shortening

1 egg slightly beaten

Insert meat thermometer into center of meat roast. Cook at 325 degrees until thermometer reaches 140 degrees (rare). Cool, wrap and refrigerate. Next day, sauté mushrooms and onion until onion is tender. Mix with liverwurst. Chill until ready to use.

To make crust mix flour, salt, parsley and celery seeds. Cut in shortening until mixture is the consistency of tiny peas. Sprinkle with cold water, 1 tablespoon at a time, tossing mixture lightly with a fork. Shape dough into a ball and roll out in a rectangle about 1/8" thick, measuring 2" wider than the length of the roast, 2" longer than its circumference. Save pastry scraps.

Remove strings from cold roast; cover top and sides of roast with the liverwurst mixture. Place roast, coated side down, on pastry rectangle. Fold up pastry to meet along center top and ends. Trim off excess pastry; moisten edges and press together firmly to seal. Place pastry covered roast, sealed edges down (Pate side is now turned up), in a greased shallow pan. Roll pastry scraps and cut out 3 flowers, 3 leaves and 3 stems. Brush pieces with beaten egg and seal to top of roast in an attractive design. Brush entire surface with beaten egg; prick with a fork. Bake at 375 for one hour or until brown. Remove roast from pan; let stand 15 minutes before carving. Makes about 12 servings.

New Orleans

When the pilot announced the final approach into New Orleans, Janelle felt like her heart stopped beating. Suddenly she had this overwhelming feeling of fear. The feeling was so foreboding that she was transfixed in her seat unable to move, even after every passenger had departed from the plane.

"Excuse me Miss," said the flight attendant. "Do you need assistance?"

Janelle quivered as if she were trying to rid herself of a terrible chill, and said, "I'm sorry, for a minute I felt so light headed and cold."

The flight attendant looked at her rather strangely and remarked, "You're probably coming down with the flu or something, because it really is quite warm in here. We turned off the air conditioning ten minutes ago."

Janelle stood up, gathered her belongings and the book Sally gave her about vampires; maybe it was the book she was reading that put this fear in her heart. She lifted her head, squared her shoulders, smiled at the stewardess and grudgingly walked off the plane.

Walking down the jet way, she tried to rationalize this feeling of dread that was still with her, when she heard her name being paged. "Excuse me," Janelle said to the very pretty blonde airline agent at the door, "I heard my name being paged."

The agent checked her notes and said, "If you are Janelle Connors, that limousine driver over in the corner was about to send out the cavalry to look for you."

Janelle laughed and thanked her, as she waved to the driver whose face turned from a deep frown to the brightest smile she had ever seen. "Ms Connors, is that you? My you sure are a lot prettier than I was told."

"Really," said Janelle, "and who told you what I looked like?"

"Uh, oh no one really Miss, it's just that anyone who's as famous a cook as you should be round and old, like my mother who works as a cook. Not someone like you, so young and pretty." As he took her small carry on bag and pointed the way to the baggage claim area, he said, "My name is Etienne. I own the limousine service and contract out for the Maison de Ville Hotel. You've never been to New Orleans before, right?"

Janelle looked at this very handsome tall Creole man of color and was astounded by his bright smile and kind eyes. She felt like she had known him for a long time, but knew that was impossible. Yet, his name sounded familiar. "No I've never been to your city before, but I have heard a lot about it from someone I used to know." Just as she said this, an uncontrollable sadness came over her, which her face could not mask. She smiled feebly and said to Etienne, "but that was a long time ago."

"Well, on the way to the hotel I will personally give you a guided tour. I'm so glad I didn't miss you! When I saw that everyone was off the plane, I began to worry."

Janelle pointed to her luggage, while Etienne scooped it up and showed the guard the luggage tag. They spent the next 30 minutes talking about the weather and how lucky she was to be in New Orleans at this time of the year, when humidity was only 40%, very low for this part of the country. He told her that in July and August you feel like your breathing in humidity, not air. She felt much more relaxed now. It seemed Etienne turned out to be a blessing with his easy way and constant prattle. He just kept her too busy to think.

The ride from the airport to the hotel was filled with facts about this wonderful town. He told her he was Creole, half black and half French, born and raised in New Orleans and knew just about everything and everyone who lived there.

When they rode by the cemetery, Etienne explained that because of the high water level and the fact that in 1718, New Orleans had been built over swampland, there were no graves below ground. There are 199 square miles of dry land; some of that land only has an elevation of 5 ft below sea level. Therefore none of the homes had basements and the dead were buried in tombs above ground; which resembled miniature houses. Janelle remarked it almost looked like a small city.

"See those brick walls around the cemetery?" asked Etienne. "They are nine feet thick and that's where they bury the less expensive interments, right into the wall.

"The only information I have about New Orleans is of the food and music," said Janelle.

At the entrance of the cemetery a funeral was in progress, with a jazz band playing loud and fast. "You like jazz music Ms Connors?"

"Oh please Etienne call me Janelle, Ms Connors is just much too formal for me. And yes, I take pride in my collection of old records by Pete Fountain, Louis Armstrong,

Dizzy Gillepsie and Thelonius Monk. Why in Germany, of all places, I even found an old record of Bessie Smith that I really treasure."

"You know Ms Janelle, Jazz was born right here in New Orleans. It is the only form of music I know of that is a combination of American Folk Music, Spanish Music, African work chants and French. It started back in the 1800's, but it was our own Louis 'Satchmo' Armstrong that made it famous throughout the world. Say now, tonight my girlfriend Angele and I are going into the French Quarter to hear a new combo in town that has combined Dixieland Jazz with Cajun music. They call it Zydeco. Would you like to join us?"

"That sounds marvelous!"

"Then it's settled. You know Ms Janelle; you're really going to like Angele. She's a business woman, like you."

"Angele owns a restaurant Etienne?"

"No maam, he laughed, "don't I wish! She can't cook a lick. She owns a Voodoo Shop in the French Quarter." He told her as he pulled up to her hotel.

"Now that's something that I have never seen! A Voodoo Shop, how interesting! Etienne, I am so glad the hotel contracts you. I can't tell you how much I have enjoyed the ride from the airport and I'm really excited about tonight."

"I'll pick you up about 8:30," he handed her luggage to the bellman, waved and drove away.

"Walking up to the front desk to register, she thought, now this just might be a fun time after all. As soon as the clerk discovered who she was, he treated her like a celebrity. She believed it had to be that southern hospitality that she had heard so much about a long time ago.

The bellman showed her to her room a beautiful one-bedroom suite. The sitting room had a beige oriental carpet that looked hand carved with colors of teal blue, pastel green, very pale pink and lilac. The drapes were a teal blue silk while the sofa and chair were a light cream. The silk pillows on the sofa entailed all the pastel colors of the carpet. It was all very elegant and quite pleasant.

Her phone rang and it was the Chairman of the committee, Mr. Harold Thodus, welcoming her to New Orleans. He told her that tomorrow there would be a press party at her hotel at four o'clock and she was to be the guest of honor.

"I'll be there," she said, "and thank you so much for the wonderful accommodations, the suite is just beautiful."

"Please don't thank me," he said. "I wish I could take credit, but your suite was prearranged by someone else."

"Please thank them for me. Oh, and I'm really looking forward to the committee's proceedings Mr. Thodus and to meeting you."

"It would be great if we could meet a few minutes earlier so that I can brief you on the schedule of events."

"Good see you tomorrow," she said, as she hung up the phone. Well she thought, in just a few hours Etienne will be picking me up. I Think I'll just relax and enjoy my surroundings until tonight.

She took a shower, turned on the television and curled up on the sofa. She hated to close her eyes; she didn't want to fall asleep. She was tired and a nap would feel good, but she was afraid she would have that same old nightmare. In spite of her fears, her eyes closed and within a few seconds she is fast asleep, and dreaming.

The dream always starts out the same, she is running as fast as she could, terrified by the sound of footsteps behind her. If only, she knew why she is running. She turns her head and screams.

Janelle woke breathing heavily, trying to catch her breath. Her heart was racing and all she can remember was that she was running from her fear. She reached for a glass of water that was sitting on the coffee table. Her hand trembled so violently she was hardly able to bring the glass to her lips. She gulped down the water with an aspirin and slowly calmed down.

Janelle checked her watch and thought, in forty minutes Etienne will be picking me up. I'm so happy I met him, she thought as the last shiver leaves her body. I just don't want to be alone tonight. She stood walked over to the closet and picked out the royal blue slack suit she had bought on Rodeo drive. There, she thought this should be appropriate for a Jazz Club, and started to dress anticipating the prospect of a good time.

Bourbon Street

Janelle checked her watch as she exited the elevator and saw Etienne with this beautiful young woman. She was just as tall as Etienne with black hair worn straight back in one long thick braid that hung down to her hips. Angele was part Portuguese, French and Nigerian. That combination of ancestors gave her skin a bronzed glow. Etienne had mentioned earlier that Angele was a runner up in the World Beauty Pageant, as Ms Haiti a few years ago. Janelle couldn't understand why she hadn't won.

Etienne walked over to her and said, "Janelle I'd like you to meet Angele."

"Angele I've heard so much about you, thank you so much for spending time with me."

"Oh, it's my pleasure, I'm sure we are going to have fun tonight."

"Etienne," Janelle whispered, "With beauty like Angele's, she doesn't need to know how to cook."

He laughed and said, "I guess your' right.

The two of them were so much fun to be around. They gave Janelle a tour of The French Quarter. The promise of darkness made Bourbon Street come alive with excitement and in all her travels, she had never seen a street as exciting as this one. Music flows from every open doorway spilling out onto the sidewalks from the many clubs. It's funny, she thought, but the merriment of the people in the streets dancing and singing to the lively Dixieland music made her feel very lonely.

They went into a club called The Cajun Café and she was amazed at the amount of people that were crammed into the lounge. They stood in the open doorway, watching the musicians and dancers, while enjoying the sound of the new music called Zydeco. It had a down hone twangy sound, more Cajun than Dixieland, but definitely a combination of the two.

On the stage were a couple of friends of Etienne's. Antoine, a slightly built handsome young man, with dark brown hair tied back into a pony tail and his wife Corinne, a large blonde woman, with long frizzy hair. The music they were playing was very lively. Antoine was strumming the fiddle and dancing all over the stage, while his wife Corinne was playing the Frottoir, a metal washboard that fitted her body like a vest. As she scraped the spoons along the ridges of the washboard, nodding her head and stamping her foot to the beat of the music, she spotted Etienne and called out "Where u at?"

"Fine," Etienne laughed. He explained to Janelle that 'where u at,' means 'how are you' in Cajun.

During intermission Janelle told Corinne how much she had enjoyed her music. "I've never learned how to play a musical instrument," she said, "but I have often admired people who do. You know Corinne it's always been one of my secret wishes to learn how to play one day."

"Well, you're just as sweet as can be. Come here mon ami, I'm going to make your wish come true." She put the vest on Janelle, and gave her a quick lesson. "O.K. you've got it now a little more rhythm, stamp your foot to the beat, good, good, c'est chaud," Corinne exclaimed.

"She says that's hot," said Etienne holding his side from laughing so hard he had to sit down.

"Now scrape those spoons to half time. That's it girl, you've got it! Janelle, you did great, maybe I'll hire you on right now."

"I did it," Janelle cried out. "I finally learned how to play a musical instrument. I know I didn't play it as well as you Corinne, but what fun. You will just have to tell me where to buy a Frottori. I want to bring it back to California with me."

She wondered why with that comment Etienne and Angele exchanged glances and smiled as if they knew a deep dark secret.

"Janelle," Angele said, "How would you like to have your future told? I have a Bocor High Priestess from Haiti appearing in my shop this week, and I would really like you to be my guest for a palm reading, or your Tarot cards read.

"I would love to meet your Bocor Priestess. How does she read your palm? It's all so mystical."

"It's more then just reading palms or cards. Quite often, if your soul is pure she is able to see many things."

The music started again, drowning out the conversation. Every one, around Janelle laughed and danced. She envied Etienne and Angele who were holding hands. They look wonderful together, and it was apparent that they are deeply in love, even though Etienne for some reason kept looking around and frowning. She wondered how is it possible to be among wall-to-wall people all having a good time, and yet feel so alone and… lost?

Someone took hold of her shoulders and swung her around. She was in the arms of a totally drunken stranger who wanted to dance. He twirled her around and around and held her so tight she couldn't breathe. As she tried to wiggle out of the embrace of this intoxicated stranger, a man gently pulled her away from him. She turned to thank him and came face to face with Beau.

She stood there totally transfixed. She wanted to speak but simply could not get her mouth to open or her vocal cords to work. When she looked into his eyes it was like floating into some abyss. He was just as handsome as ever and she wondered if her chest could contain her rapidly beating heart. She shook her head and forced herself to speak.

"Hello Beau, it's been a long time," she said in a low whisper, as she tried to catch her breath.

At Last

For a moment the artist in him took over. He studied her face, not wanting to miss any detail; even the slightest difference was noted. She seemed to be frozen in time. It had been years since he last saw her, yet every line of her face was just the same. He longed to touch her with his lips to feel the softness of her full mouth. Just thinking about it awakens his body with desire for her. Even after all this time, nothing had changed one iota. In his eyes she was so beautiful. He wished he could erase the past and take her in his arms. Instead he had to make polite conversation while every fiber of his body was screaming out to touch her, hold her, and never let her go.

Finally he found his voice, "Janelle, how wonderful to see you here in New Orleans. You are just as beautiful as the last time I saw you." He held a tight grip on her, fearing she might disappear if he let go, as he walked her away from the crowd. "Do you mind," he said. "I would love to buy you a drink. I know this little bar that is about a block away on the corner of Dauphine and Toulouse. It's very quite there and we have a lot of catching up to do." He turned to thank a smiling Etienne for taking care of Janelle. "Oh," she whispered, "of course he's your old friend."

As they walked through the narrow old streets he heard

the flutter of wings from a few pigeons that had been startled by their footsteps. To him, it almost sounded like the wings of angels, for there must be an angel watching over him, bringing her back into his life.

She was confused; did Beau know all along that she was coming to New Orleans? It seemed he knew she would be in the French Quarter tonight. There were so many questions flying around in her brain. Were her legs really moving? Or was she floating beside him. I'm so grateful, she thought, that he is holding my hand so tight; I don't think I could function if he ever let it go.

As they walked, she could smell the succulent aroma of Cajun cooking that is only associated with this old world city. The air was filled with the aroma and the sensuous sounds of trumpets that were embracing them, wrapping them in the warmth of the soulful tune. Her senses filled with the magic of the music, the aroma, and Beau.

The bar that Beau took her to was dark, quiet and exquisitely furnished. The soft piano music playing in the background was perfect for two old lovers that hadn't seen each other in quite some time. Beau ordered a bottle of Don Perignom and the waiter made quite a fuss in serving it. Nothing is too good for Janelle, thought Beau more then ever he knew she was the one for him, and this time he won't let anyone or anything stand in his way

When he looked at her he felt alive again. The years that had passed without her seemed like a dream.

He lifted his glass and said, "To us," while looking deeply into her eyes. He felt sad thinking of all the time wasted when he could have had her by his side sharing his life. He loved being with her. She was very exciting and intelligent; it saddened him when he thought of those precious years he had to live without her near him.

He stared at her face, and asked, "Why Janelle? Why didn't you answer any of my letters? I wrote you, sometimes twice a day, until my letters were returned to me unopened. I called and left message after message. Then after a while, I thought it was hopeless and just got on with my life."

"Beau, I saw you with Mala and it was like a knife going into my heart. I was told the two of you were engaged."

"Who told you that? Engaged to Mala? You have got to be kidding! She of all people! Never, never in a million years."

"It was her friend Sandra who told me, I believed her because I saw you in bed with her. Oh Beau it seemed that in just three days my life changed drastically. My parents died in an automobile accident the same night I walked in on you and Mala. You never came to see me when they took me to the hospital, or to the funeral of my parents. What was I to think? I was crushed; I just didn't understand the deception. Why pretend you loved me when it was Mala all along."

He took out a typed report from his breast pocket, carefully unfolded it, moved the candle closer to her and said, "Please read this Janelle. It explains everything. You'll see that I was set up."

She read the report Gus sent to Beau from the laboratory. It was dated that awful week, so many years ago, and described a drug called GHQ, that was found in his bloodstream.

"I saved the report Janelle, and always carried it with me. I never lost hope that someday I would see you again, and I would be able to prove that I had been drugged for three of the longest days of my life."

As she read the report tears were streaming down her face, tears of sadness because of time lost, and tears of joy for finding each other again. He didn't want Mala after all. He wasn't responsible for those awful days.

93

"Oh Beau," she sighed as she rubbed her forehead hoping to chase away all the confusion, "we have a lot of catching up to do."

He reached across the table, took her hand and pressed it to his lips. "Yes Janelle, we certainly do, starting right now."

Laissez Lees Ben Temps Roller

It was one of those perfect weather days, she thought as she sat with Beau at an outdoor café on Decature and St Philip in the Vieu Carr. The ambiance of the wrought iron table and chairs under the canopy gave the feeling of being an observer of life.

Listening to the wonderful Jazz music, from the small combo a few feet away, while lunching on a muffuletta sandwich and sipping a cool drink called Cookery Hurricane, was very relaxing. It was fun to watch the crowds of people going in and out of the shops and restaurants; New Orleans was just so full of life.

Janelle and Beau sipped their drinks as the musicians finished their rendition of an old Louis Armstrong tune, 'When It's Sleepy Time Down South.' Everyone applauded, as the band started to play, 'When The Saints Go Marching In,' a favorite song of the many musicians in New Orleans.

Janelle noticed an elderly woman sitting alone at the corner table. It was apparent that she was overweight and her legs were not what they once were, as she slowly eased her body from the chair. She opened her soiled imitation blue silk umbrella and proceeded to dance while twirling the handle of the umbrella. She swung her hips to the rhythm of the music as strands of her slightly yellowish gray hair fell across her crocodiled lined face.

She entertained the patrons sitting in the open café, but she wasn't dancing for them, no not at all, it was for herself. She was reliving a time she remembered so long ago when she was young and pretty and could dance all night on Bourbon Street. As she swayed and turned to the beat of the music swinging her old blue and pink faded print skirt, Janelle noticed the look on her face was pure euphoria. She knew this woman wasn't here in this café, mentally, she was in another time, another place. She was feeling the music, as one would feel a soft breeze or falling snow. Even if there wasn't any music playing, she still would have gotten up and danced. For the music she hears is deep in her heart, and she loved every minute of it.

When the song ended, Janelle watched the old woman close the umbrella and walk back to her table. She sat alone sipping her strong coffee and washing it down with small swallows of ice water. The woman sat smiling for in spite of her inexpensive clothing she was happy. She knew that this woman was living her life her way, and even the aching legs and the obvious age couldn't stop her from dancing.

Beau called the waiter over and asked him to bring the woman some appetizers and a frozen drink.

"For Ms Em, Mr. Beau?" asked the waiter. "Why I know she would really appreciate that. I'll bring her a frozen Tropical Spellbinder and her favorite appetizer Shrimp Remoulade."

"Such exotic drinks you serve," said Janelle to the waiter. "What is a Tropical Spellbinder?"

"Well, we take a little absolute citron, some vodka, a splash of blue curacao, some midori and top it off with a cherry," he said.

"I've got to write this down," said Janelle. "I don't want to forget it, it sounds great."

"Yes maam it seems Ms Em likes them a whole lot," he laughed. "You know Ms Em comes to the café with her umbrella quite often and always alone. She once told me that everyone she was close to is gone, but when she hears the music she can feel her loved ones around her once again. She always dances to the tune of When The Saints Go Marching In. She told me it reminds her of someone special she used to know."

When the old woman was served she raised her glass to them and said, "Laissez Les Bon Temps Rouler!"

"Tell me what she said Beau."

"She said 'Let the good times roll." He laughed, "And she sure does."

"Yes, perhaps she's right," said Janelle rather pensively, listening to the story the waiter told them about Ms Em had touched Janelle's heart. "No matter what your circumstances in life are or how many obstacles you have to overcome, it is important to savor the good times when they come along. Like now Beau right this minute, for you and me, these are part of our good time, for we don't know what tomorrow holds for us."

"Of course you're right Janelle. We have lost time that we should have shared together. No more lost time for us. We are going to live life to the fullest starting right now. Come; let me show you the French Quarter. I'm taking you on a tour, and no one knows this town like I do."

Spending these last few days with Beau had brought back all the old feelings that had lain dormant within her. Long ago she had buried how she felt about him so deeply she never thought these feelings would ever surface again. He made her heart feel like it was going to burst with happiness.

"We're going to walk to Jackson Square, its only one block from here," he said as he took her hand, "that's where the French Quarter first started. This section of New Orleans is like what the Casbah is to Algiers."

"The original neighborhood is the French Quarter, or Sier de Bienvile. Its French founder and his convict salt smugglers cleared the land and were the first settlers. The colony consisted of convicts straight from debtor's prison, and women from the streets of Paris." He put his arm around her waist as he escorted her across the street. "Now this section is filled with artists sketching tourists, musicians on every corner, tee shirt shops, dance clubs, bars and strip joints."

"Around the corner is St. Louis Cathedral, the oldest cathedral in the United States. It was built in 1722, destroyed by fire and rebuilt in 1845. The church is now a landmark, and is known for its magnificent stained glass murals. Right now it is over run with many priests and nuns that have come here on a pilgrimage from all over the country. They are praying day and night that they win the war."

"The war, what war?"

"Why the war they are fighting against the termites. These buildings are hundreds of years old and are very close to collapsing because of the termites that have invaded New Orleans."

"I hope the nuns win, it would be a shame to destroy so much history."

Beau pointed to the horse and buggies that hugged the curb on Decatur Street. "How about, a horse and buggy ride? Well, actually the horses are half mule and half horse. We find that they are sturdier than full bred horses for pulling carriages."

"They sure look cute with the way the horses and

buggies are decorated with flowers and ribbons. As a matter of fact everything here is so festive looking, like one big party that never ends."

"That's my town," exclaimed Beau, "come we'll ride for a while. Driver, take us by the LaLaurie house. Now tell me Janelle, to you believe in ghosts?"

"Ghosts, well Beau let's put it this way, I have never seen a ghost, nor do I want to, but I don't disbelieve."

"Smart girl, I will tell you the story of Marie Delphine Mc Carty Lalaurie. Her house was built in 1831 at 1140 Royal Street. Delphine Lalaurie was very glamorous, but quite mad. She allegedly chained and starved her slaves until several of them committed suicide. When her neighbors heard of her conduct, they formed a mob to rescue the slaves and kill her. She heard of their plan and escaped to Europe where she stayed until the end of her life, too afraid to ever set foot in her home again. Till this day there are many people who swear they hear screams and groans coming from this house in the middle of the night."

"Wait driver," Beau called out, "stop over by Aunt Sally's Shop. You are going to love this Janelle. Come look around the gift shop while I pick up some Creole Pralines, they are a sugary treat you won't forget."

Janelle was impressed with the little gift shop. She purchased some recipe cards on Creole cooking, and Aunt Sally's recipe for Pecan Pralines that she just loved. As they climbed back into the buggy, she said, "Beau, I'm so glad I now have Aunt Sally's recipe for my customers back in Crestview." After saying this she thought, how am I ever going to exist without Beau in my life? She knew that she must deal with this problem, but not now, not today. Maybe she would think about it tomorrow.

"Now Janelle, this is St. Peters Street, where we have

the French Market. Here, we sell fresh fruits and vegetables, even long sugar canes from the field. It's hard to believe that over 200 years ago this area had ships unloading cargo from exotic ports all over the world. It is written that the air always smelled of strong coffee from Brazil, fresh flowers from the Caribbean and frying fish. On the weekends you'll find a lot of entrepreneurs setting up their booths and selling everything from leather purses and wallets to antiques, ceramic masks and dresses.

"Your city, is surrounded by music, it is the breath of life. Even in this section there are outdoor cafes and live bands playing wonderful melodies. Everywhere people are eating marvelous food, drinking exotic drinks and dancing to the sounds of this great town. It is teeming with life and yes, the good times."

"See that cornstalk fence over there? Well this is a true love story. The woman who lived here at 915 Royal Street, missed her home town in the Midwest so much, that her husband had a wrought iron corn stalk fence made and shipped by sea from Philadelphia to make her feel less homesick."

"Over there," he said, "at 1113 Chartres is the Beauregard House built in 1827. The Confederate General PGT Beauregard rented a room there, as did Francis Parkinson Keyes."

"It's all so amazing, Janelle remarked. "These buildings are so old, filled with so much history. If you close your eyes and listen to the clip clop of the horse you can almost visualize the way it was one hundred years ago."

Beau never ceased to be amazed at the dept of this beautiful woman who was sitting beside him. Her ability to have other people and places enter into her life, to become completely absorbed with their culture, simply amazed him. It was as easy for her as breathing air. He was convinced that she had that rare gift of being able to fit in anywhere.

"You can stop in front of the Maison De Ville Hotel, driver. Here we are Janelle, your press party is about to begin." News reporters came running as Beau lifted Janelle down from the buggy, while flash bulbs were popping and questions were shouted at Janelle. The press conference went very well. They asked Janelle many questions about the restaurant and about her recipes.

"Our town," remarked a young reporter "is filled with wonderful chefs. What makes your restaurant so unique to win such a prestigious award?"

"Oh, I don't think my restaurant is any better than what is available right here. When I think about why I have won this award, I believe the combination of the panoramic view, along with the unusual ever changing menus," Janelle smiled, "has a lot to do with it. Let me explain that comment," she said. "I have learned from experience what does or does not work in creating an interesting menu. For instance it sounds so ordinary to list on your menu, 'included with an entrée is a choice of soup or salad.' It is my opinion that if re-worded, just a touch, it sounds so much more appealing to the senses to say, also served with your entrée is a choice of Chef's soup of the day or Endive Radicchio Salad with sliced almonds and house dressing or Virgin Olive Oil and Balsamic vinegar."

"However, there is one item that I will definitely add to my menu after experiencing life here in New Orleans, and that's your wonderful Alligator Soup."

After these comments the reporters were all very complimentary toward Janelle. Beau smiled, as he watched them fussing over her, he knew that with this one comment, she won over every reporter there.

Mr. Thodus was standing right beside Janelle during the press party. After forty minutes of questions, he smiled, held up his hands, and said to the reporters, "I really think that you have taken enough pictures and asked enough questions for today. We would like to thank you all for coming. Of course you're invited to the reception tomorrow night. I know you will definitely enjoy the dinner," he laughed. "Thank you all again," he said, as he took Janelle arm and escorted her into the hotel.

"Most people," Mr. Thodus said to Janelle, "are intimidated by the press. I am very impressed with the way you handled the reporters.

Janelle blushed, and said, "I'm sure it's because of your moral support."

He shook her hand and said, "Thanks again Ms. Connors, I'm looking forward to tomorrow night, but now I must run and take care of a few last minute details."

"Oh Beau, I'm so glad you were here for me, I was so nervous."

"I think from now on you're going to have a little bit of trouble getting rid of me, I'll always be here for you." He looked at her and thought tomorrow night is the Reception in the Mardi Gras Ballroom; the invitation list looked like the who's who of New Orleans. Everyone of any importance would be there from the Governor on down, even my parents. I will be proud to introduce her to New Orleans Society, but oh how I wish I could I could be alone with her tonight. I'm aching to take her into my arms, to caress her body and never ever let her go.

Janelle touched his handsome face, and said, "Beau this has been such a busy day, would you mind very much if we didn't go out for dinner? If maybe we could stay in my suite and order Room Service?"

Beau sighed, and said, "I swear you must have been reading my mind."

"It's just that we haven't had a chance to talk," said Janelle, "and I would really like to know what you've been doing with your life these last few years."

He took her hand and together they walked into the hotel.

New Orleans Shrimp Remoulade

3 eggs

¼ cup Creole mustard or whole grain mustard

2 tbs. red wine vinegar

2 tbs. Worcestershire sauce

2 celery stalks, coarsely chopped

¼ cup minced parsley, preferably flat-leaf

1 tsp. salt

1-1/2 tsp. Tabasco sauce

Boston lettuce leaves

Lemon wedges

Curly leaf parsley sprigs

2-½ lbs. Shelled, cleaned boiled medium shrimp, well chilled

¼ cup ballpark style mustard

½ cup ketchup

¼ cup prepared horseradish

1 tbs. paprika

3 large garlic cloves, minced

2 bay leaves, minced

juice of 1 medium lemon

½ cup good quality olive oil

In a food processor fitted with the steel blade, combine eggs. Creole mustard, ballpark style mustard, ketchup, vinegar, horseradish, Worcestershire sauce, paprika, celery, garlic, parsley, bay leaves, salt, lemon juice and Tabasco sauce. Process until smooth. With machine running, pour oil through feed tube in a slow, steady stream, processing to form a smooth emulsion. To serve, arrange shrimp on lettuce leaves and top generously with sauce. Garnish plates with parsley sprigs and lemon wedges. Make 4 to 6 servings.

Muffuletta Bread

1 cup of warm water (110F)	1 tbs. of sugar
1 (1/4 oz.) pkg. Active dry yeast	1 tbs. sesame seeds
About 3 cups bread flour	1 ½ tsp. salt
2 tbs. vegetable shortening	1 tbs. sesame seeds

In a 2-cup glass-measuring cup, combine water and sugar. Stir in yeast. Let stand until foamy, 5 to 10 minutes. In a food processor fitted with the steel blade, combine 3 cups flour, salt and shortening. Add yeast mixture. Process until dough forms a ball, about 5 seconds. Stop machine; check consistency of dough. It should be smooth and satiny. If dough is too dry, add more warm water, 1 tbs. at a time, processing just until blended. Process, 20 seconds to knead. Lightly oil a large bowl, swirling to coat bottom and sides. Place dough in oiled bowl; turn to coat all sides. Cover bowl with plastic wrap. Let rise in a warm, draft free place until doubled in bulk, about 1- ½ hours. Lightly grease a baking sheet. When dough has doubled in bulk punch down dough; turn out onto a lightly floured surface. Form dough into a round loaf about 10 inches in diameter; place on greased baking sheet sprinkle top of loaf with sesame seeds; press seeds gently into surface of loaf. Cover very loosely with plastic wrap; let rise until almost doubled in bulk, 1 hour. Place rack in center of oven. Preheat oven 425 F. Remove plastic wrap. Bake loaf in center of preheated oven 10 minutes. Reduce heat to 375F; bake 25 minutes. The loaf is done when it sounds hollow when tapped on bottom. Cool completely on a rack before slicing. Makes 1 loaf.

Muffuletta Sandwich

1 (10-inch) Muffuletta Bread loaf
2 oz. Capocollo, thinly sliced
2 oz. Provolone cheese, thinly sliced
2 oz. Genoa salami, thinly sliced
2 oz. Prosciutto, thinly sliced
1 cup Olive Salad

A muffuletta is a New Orleans sandwich extravaganza of Italian meats and cheeses, lavishly spread with olive salad and stuffed between a seeded bun the size of a dinner plate.

Cut bread in half crosswise. Pile several layers of salami, capocollo, prosciutto, over bottom layer. Add layers of cheese. Top with Olive Salad and cover with top portion of bread. Press down slightly. Cut sandwich in quarters. Use wooden picks to secure layers. Makes 1 to 4 servings depending on the appetite.

Olive Salad

1 32 oz. Jar broken green olives (unstuffed)
6 garlic cloves, minced
1 cup marinated cocktail onions, drained
4 celery stalks, halved lengthwise
1/3- cup olive oil
1-4oz. Jar chopped pimentos drained
1 tbs. dried leaf oregano
1 tsp. finely ground pepper
3 tbs. red wine vinegar

Drain olives, reserve 3 tbs. brine. In a medium bowl, combine olives, garlic, onions, celery, and pimentos. In a small bowl, whisk reserved olive brine, oregano pepper and vinegar until combined. Add olive oil in a slow, steady stream, whisking constantly. Pour dressing over salad; toss. Spoon into a jar, with a tight fitting lid. Refrigerate until served or up to 3 weeks. Serve at room temperature. Makes about 5 cups.

The Supper

Beau wanted this dinner to be special, he had been dreaming of being alone with Janelle for such a long time. He called room service, and spent fifteen minutes planning the meal with the head chef. He ordered a salad with chopped walnuts, Steak Diane, and Cherries Jubilee. Beau opened the bottle of imported champagne that Janelle had on ice. He poured them two drinks and made small talk until the waiter was through setting up the table with exquisite crystal glasses and china dinnerware.

All of a sudden they were alone and became shy with each other. This was the first time that they were alone. She remarked about the weather, and how warm it was for December. He told her that it is not uncommon for it to snow at anytime, but it doesn't really last long at this time of the year.

"I really liked the way you handled the reporters," he said trying to overcome the uncomfortable silence that had engulfed them. "What happened to that scared girl I use to know? I remember how uncertain you always were of yourself. Well you certainly have come a long way."

Janelle blushed, took a sip of wine, as the waiters finished placing the dinner on the table. When he dimmed the lights, the glow from the floating candles in the brandy snifter and the soft classical music in the background gave off a very romantic feeling. Beau tipped the waiters, and escorted them to the door. He poured more champagne, as they sat at the beautifully prepared dinner table.

"This looks wonderful, everything is perfect," Janelle said as she reached across the table to squeeze his hand. "I'm so glad you also wanted a quite dinner. I've been very curious about your life Beau, tell me what have you been doing since I last saw you in Crestview?"

"Let's see…where do I start?"

"From the beginning," she smiled, "and don't leave anything out."

He took a sip of champagne, thought a moment, and said, "From the beginning, of course, I was devastated when I couldn't find you. I tried everything. I called Sally constantly but she wouldn't tell me anything. I wrote letters to you, in care of Mary, and they were returned to me, unopened. I thought you were lost to me. So I did the only thing I could do to forget the pain of losing you, I threw myself into my work. Every ounce of energy went into my causes."

"Tell me about the causes," said Janelle as she handed Beau the basket of hot bread.

He finished his salad and remarked about how good it was. Taking a bite of steak, he rolled his eyes and moaned with pleasure.

Janelle laughed at his antics and said, "Come on now, quit stalling and tell me about your causes?"

"After I came back from California, I gave some serious thoughts about my future. I realized the importance of various vocations and decided to go on to law school."

"Then you're a lawyer?"

"Not quite. You know it's no secret that I come from a

wealthy family. My father did very well with what his father and grand-father had left him."

"Your family is in cotton, right?"

"Yeah cotton, a nice stable business. We didn't grow it; we just owned mills that refined it. From generation to generation it's always the same, possibly a few updates with technology, but all in all, the mills almost run themselves. I couldn't see myself feeling fulfilled by working my entire life in the mills." He took the last bite of his steak, finished the wine in his glass and sighed.

"So that's why you chose to study law?" she asked, as she poured the coffee.

"Exactly, I took a good look around me; I mean a really good look and realized that not everyone was as fortunate as I. One night in particular, my friends and I were in a heated discussion about welfare. Everyone complains that welfare is wrong but no one does anything about it. My friends were saying it should stop. The people receiving these handouts should take care of themselves, instead of depending on the state. In other words get a job."

"Continue," she said, you have my complete attention. I want to hear the rest of this story."

"Ok, I agreed to a point that they should get a job, but it's just not that cut and dry."

There was a knock on the door, Beau pushed his chair back, stood and went to open the door. A waiter entered, cleared away the dinner dishes and reset the table for desert. He flamed the Cherries Jubilee and left them to enjoy the treat.

"This is great," Janelle said as she took a bite of the cherries. "I must have the recipe for this dish."

"That could very easily be arranged, since the Chef is a friend of mine."

"Of course he is," Janelle laughed. "Everyone in this town is a friend of yours."

His eyes twinkled, as he grinned with pleasure. "Now, I believe we were talking about welfare and its problems?"

"Your right we were. Well, Beau continued, "sometimes people on welfare think this is the only way they can survive. Minimum wage jobs, after taxes leaves them with less than food stamps and welfare. Medical benefits are not available when working at a fast food restaurant."

"That's right."

"When people are untrained, they lose confidence in their ability to function on their own and become unemployable. So the answer lies in rehabilitation. We need workshops to train men and women, giving them the opportunity to become employed in any one of a number of occupations: such as truck drivers, bricklayers and computer data processors. They just need training. Welfare should be used as a temporary remedy, not a permanent one. There are families that are third generation welfare recipients. This is the only way of life they know."

"How sad, when you're caught in that mode, you'll never realize your full potential. They will never know how satisfying it is to accomplish something you never thought you could do."

"That's exactly what some of us thought. We all put our heads together and came up with a format. We thought that welfare should only be offered for a period of say six months, enough time for training and job placement. Of course the people on it would be monitored for attendance. If they don't show up for training, a week's benefits should be deducted from their checks."

"Sure, why not?" she said, "That sounds fair."

"Of course every new program is bound to have draw backs. First we started contacting the leaders of this town.

The most influential businessmen gave us donations, for equipment so that we could start the workshops. We got them involved and it was fun for all of us."

"It sounds like fun."

"My father donated a building where we set one room aside for a nursery. Parents could have their children taken care of while they're in a training class. We had senior citizens donating their time to take care of the children and we would provide them free lunches that were donated by local restaurants."

"Great planning did it work?"

"Not only did it work, but we discovered ways to expand the program. We found that poverty shows no favoritism; it could affect anyone of every race. In just four years we found employment for about six thousand people, from every walk of life."

"Yes, its true, misfortune could happen to anyone."

"The largest population suffering were, the Cajuns, living near by in the Bayou. Nearly one thousand Cajuns had fishing restrictions imposed on them and to make matters worse the petroleum recession also added to the lack of work. We found employment for most of them, and they were not placed in fast food minimum wage type jobs either. The jobs paid decent wages and included benefits."

"You must know that if it wasn't for your accomplishments they would still be poor," she said as she pushed away her half eaten desert.

"Well to continue, by the time I graduated from law school, I knew just about everyone in this town, rich and poor. Because of my efforts, I was asked to run for the office of Attorney General and I won. I've had this job for a year and next year, to my surprise, I've been asked to run for Congress."

"That's wonderful! I envy you Beau. You must be very proud of your life, hmm," she said as she reflected for a moment, "It's all so interesting."

"What is? Come on tell me what you are thinking."

"Well it's just that sometimes life deals you blows that you thought were so devastating, only to discover years later that if they hadn't happen, you never would have made it to the point where you are now. I'm so happy for you. You're successful, doing something with your life to better those around you." She took a sip of water, looked up and said, "You did well with you life, Beau, and I'm very happy for you."

"Speaking of accomplishments Janelle," he said as he pushed his chair closer to her. "What about you? Look at where you are now compared to that barefoot overworked girl I used to know. You are being honored by your peers with a very prestigious award."

Beau looked at her lovely face, took her hand and said, "I hope you won't be angry with me, but I do have a confession to make to you. When the newspaper came out with the contest that the Association was giving, I submitted the name of your restaurant. You see I've been keeping track of you from afar. I thought you would at least attend the ceremony and I'd get a chance to see you again. I was just delighted when I heard you had won. I swear to you I had nothing to do with it. You won the award entirely on your own merit."

"It's nice to know you've been thinking of me," she said as she kissed the tip of his nose and then put her eyes down and blushed.

He sensed the awkwardness between them and thought perhaps they should leave the room. He pushed her hair back from her forehead and said, "Janelle would you like to go for a walk?"

"That might be a good idea," she sighed nervously. She went to the coffee table, picked up her purse and walked to the door. As she turned to flick the light switch off, she brushed against Beau who stood behind her. She turned to say something to him, but her words were lost when she looked into his eyes.

The air was filled with her fragrance; even her hair had the clean smell of summer. Her perfume intoxicated him more then the wind did. He bent to kiss her, at first so tenderly and softly, slowly building into a sweet, intense passion that surprised them both. Neither one wanted to stop. She kissed his forehead, his eyes, and every inch of his face while he just wanted to devour her neck as he unbuttoned her blouse and she slipped out of her camisole. Although the light was dim, he noticed the contrast of her milky white breast, the rosy pink of her firm nipples with the contrast of her California tan. He couldn't help himself, his mouth closed over her nipple while he sucked them harder and harder. He just couldn't get enough of her. She felt so soft and sweet, he dreamt of this moment for so many years. He wasn't sure how long he would be able to restrain himself, for every inch of his body felt like it was on fire.

She too was in ecstasy, for never before had she felt such bliss. "Oh Beau," she sobbed, "I've missed you so much. I'm so glad you found me."

He led her to the bed, as both of them slipped out of their clothes and lay down together. He took her into his arms and said, "Janelle you know I have always loved you. I guess I realized it that day on the beach, six years ago when I first held you in my arms. I knew then, there would never be anyone else but you. He sighed deeply as he kissed her, on the lips, then her cheeks, her neck her breasts; every inch of her body was awakened by his touch. "I just knew someday, somehow," he whispered, "we would be together again. We were meant for each other, soul mates forever. I promise I will never lose you again."

She moaned with sheer pleasure, tears of joy streamed down her face, as they made passionate love until the wee hours of the morning. They talked in-between their love making, as their hands explored and caressed each other's bodies.

Over and over again they lost themselves in each other's arms, while their bodies responded to their passion. Exhausted, Beau looked at the clock and moaned, "Oh no it's four o'clock." He kissed her and lovingly explained that he had to leave. "Janelle it kills me to leave you now, but I have an early morning meeting that I just can't break. Now that I have found you again, I swear to you that soon, very soon we'll spend the rest of our lives together."

"I know I feel the same way. Tomorrow, oh I guess its today; I promised Angele I would visit her shop. She wants me to meet her High Priestess from Haiti. I'm looking forward to it; it should all be very interesting. I also want to browse the antique stores on Royal Street. With such a busy schedule, I hope I have enough time to spend a couple of hours primping for the ball. I do want to look my best so you would be proud of me."

He stood at the open door, frowned and very seriously said, "I will always be proud to have you by my side," as he blew her a kiss and left the room.

She reveled in the ecstasy of him as she drifted off to sleep hugging his pillow. Within minutes the nightmare began. She felt as though she were choking, she couldn't breathe. She saw herself terrified and running, not knowing why, only that she must get away! She looked back, and saw a man with a gun, as she tripped and fell. She turned her head, looked into his horrible black, cold eyes, and screamed.

She bolted up in bed, drenched in perspiration, shaking with fear. "Oh Beau," she cried, "I need you as she hugged his pillow!"

Walnut Salad

1 clove of garlic
2 qts. Mixed greens (spinach, leaf lettuce, bib lettuce
    endive and celery)
1 qt, head lettuce
1-$\frac{1}{2}$ tsp. salt
$\frac{3}{4}$ tsp. freshly ground peppercorns
$\frac{1}{2}$ cup salad oil
4 tbsp. Creole mustard
4 tbsp. wine vinegar
$\frac{1}{2}$ cup walnut halves
Rub salad bowl with crushed garlic clove and discard

Break dry salad greens into small pieces before measuring (do not cut them). Sprinkle salt and pepper over greens in bowl. Add salad oil, turn with fork until leaves are coated with oil. Mix mustard and wine vinegar. Pour over greens just before serving. Toss lightly. Add $\frac{1}{2}$ cup walnuts. Makes 12 servings.

Creole Mustard

1-$\frac{1}{4}$ cups of stone ground mustard
2/3-cup mayonnaise
4 tsp. prepared horseradish
$\frac{1}{4}$ tsp red cayenne pepper

In a small bowl, whisk all ingredients until combined. Cover and refrigerate until chilled before serving. Makes about 2 cups.

Steak Diane

2 ten -ounce sirloin steaks
3 tbsp. salted butter
2 tbsp. sweet butter
2 tsp. chopped chives
4 tbsp. sherry
2 tbsp. cognac, heated

Trim the meat well and pound very thin with a mallet. Heat three tablespoons of salted butter in a chafing dish platter. Add the steak and cook quickly, turning it once. Add the cognac and flame. Add the sherry and the sweet butter creamed with chives. Place the steak on a warm platter and pour the pan juices over it.

Cherries Jubilee

1 can pitted black cherries
$\frac{1}{4}$ cup warmed kirsch or cognac
1 tbsp. sugar
1 tbsp. cornstarch
Vanilla ice cream

Drain the cherries, reserving the juice. Mix the sugar with the cornstarch and add one cup of the reserved juice, a little at a time. Cook three minutes, stirring constantly. Add the cherries and pour the kirsch over the top. Ignite the kirsch and ladle the sauce over the cherries. Serve over vanilla ice cream.

Rage

As Mala scanned the front page of the early morning news-paper, she saw the picture of a smiling Beau lifting Janelle off of the horse and buggy. Janelle looked so beautiful with her long curly red hair blowing in the wind. The newspaper shook, as Mala stared at the picture of Beau firmly gripping Janelle's waist. The rage that overcame her was uncontrol-lable. She screamed and ripped the newspaper to shreds.

"That little bitch! That stupid waitress is back! What is it about her that he likes? I don't get it! She's nothing, a little nothing red headed bitch!"

Bits of newspaper flew across the room. She picked up a glass of juice and flung it, barely missing the window, as it smashed against the wall. The orange stain slowly slid down the wall, marking a testimony of her rage.

"It's always been her," she screamed. "I'll fix her once and for all! Just watch me, I'll do it." She paced back and forth like a caged animal repeating over and over, "I'll do it! I'll get rid of her," she shouted as she pushed over a chair. "Watch and see, I'll fix her but good, this time!"

Her face became a mask of hatred as her father; the most feared man in New Orleans entered the room, and saw the results her rage has caused. Observing the chaos, from her behavior, it was as if he had been thrust back in time and was watching his wife for Mala was the exact image of her.

"Not again," he sighed, "it's too much to bear in one lifetime. First my wife and now my only child has gone mad." He shuddered as he felt his heart breaking. Deep down, he had always felt responsible for the death of his wife. He thought he could make it up to his daughter by giving her everything she wanted. He hoped it would make her happy.

When Mala had told him about her obsession to marry Beau, he did everything short of murder to convince Beau to be with Mala. I am a feared man in this town, he thought, they don't call me Tyler the Terrible behind my back for nothing. I've earned that title, and I'm proud of it. I've destroyed more lives then I can count with my power, but Beau was someone I could not touch. He and his father are too well liked; they have many old family ties with other powerful people.

Once he tried to manipulate Beau by threatening to plunge the stock of the cotton mills, and force Beau's father John into bankruptcy. That didn't prove successful because someone on his staff alerted Beau and the plan fell apart. There is a shield that protects this family, by all their friends, both rich and poor.

Mala looked up and noticed her father standing in the doorway and immediately pounced on him screaming and pounding on his chest with her fists. "I want her dead, do you hear me? I want her dead! Fix it! You could do it! Kill her!"

He looked at her, while tears welled up in his eyes. He too had seen the picture in the newspaper, and had hurried over to comfort his daughter. He knew she would be devastated but he just didn't know to what extent.

"Do you hear me or are your deaf? I said I want you to kill her!"

"No Mala," he whispered. "I can't do that."

"Yes you can," she screamed. "I want her dead!"

"No. That's a word I should have said to you a long time ago."

She started hitting him, and yelling, "I hate you, I've always hated you. You have never been there for me, not ever!"

He grabbed her by the shoulders and shook her, "Listen to me," he said. "This is one time I must draw the line, I will not do this. I have given you everything all your life, but I won't give you this."

She looked up at him, her face filled with vile hatred, as she yelled, "You've given me nothing! You've never given me anything I wanted."

"You know that's not true. After you finished school in California and you wanted to become a high fashion model, didn't I use my connections so that you would be seen in every fashion magazine? Your beauty has made you famous."

"I only wanted fame, so that Beau would desire me, so that he would love me. Don't you see nothing matters to me if I don't have him? It's all, your fault that he doesn't want me. It's because of your underhanded way of making money. That's all you ever cared about, making money, no matter who gets hurt."

"Come with me," he said trying to take her arm, as she violently pushed him away. "We could take a trip. We could go to Paris tonight. You like Paris, don't you?"

Mala said nothing, but continued to pace back and forth like a caged animal.

"Or maybe we could go to the beach house in Florida. Forget about him, I could get you a hundred other young men much better than Beau Rampart; yes that's it, I'll introduce you to others."

Mala just stared at him with narrowed eyes that were filled with hatred.

"I'll contact my associates in Florida, we'll plan a party. I'll invite every client that has a son; all the richest bachelors will be there. You'll see, you won't even remember Beau, after you meet them."

"I told you, I want her dead," Mala said menacingly. "If you won't do this for me, then I'll do it myself. After all, why should you be the only one who destroys lives, I am of your blood and I've learned a lot from you. I want him," she screamed, "don't you understand? It's always been him, no one else will ever do!"

He took a step toward her to take her in his arms and somehow comfort her.

She pushed him away, pointed her neatly manicured finger at him and said very seriously, "I'll kill her myself, wait and see. I heard it's easy to kill someone, I'll do it, and then he'll be mine, or no one's." She turned very quickly and ran out of the house to her car.

"Mala wait, please wait. I'll fix it, I promise," he yelled after her, but it was too late. As he reached the porch he could hear the squeal of the tires of the red Jaguar as it raced out of the driveway and onto the street.

He watched the car disappear down the road, as an overwhelming sadness came over him. Suddenly his body went limp, he collapsed on the front steps hugging his knees as he lowered his head onto his arms, and for the first time in his entire life, Tyler the Terrible cried uncontrollably.

The Warning

A few short blocks from Janelle's hotel sat Angele's quaint voodoo shop. Janelle heard a very mystical melody from the door chimes as she entered.

"Janelle how wonderful to see you again," said a smiling Angele, as she came from behind the counter and embraced her new friend.

"I love your shop, and look at you, don't you look stunning in your long print colorful dress, and that matching turban is just great."

"Oh this is just my uniform so to speak, I have to look the part in my magical surroundings. You know the customers expect it."

'You browse while I do a little business." Janelle was amazed at how quickly Angele's speech had become laced with a thick Haitian accent. I guess it goes with the uniform she thought, Etienne is right she is a smart business- woman.

The dim lighting only enhanced the eerie atmosphere of the store. The walls and ceiling were covered in a deep purple with hand painted sacred Voodoo symbols. She saw huge African masks in every corner painted in vibrant colors.

One whole wall was filled with Voodoo Dolls of different shapes and sizes. Some dolls were made of stuffed cotton, while others were of straw covered by a cotton print shirt and pants or dress. Each doll had a small pouch and a tag attached to it. One said love, another success, good fortune, how to meet a man, how to keep your man, how to get even with your boss, and many more.

On the tag were instructions. She read; In order to fulfill your wish you must light a candle, place a lock of hair, a small picture, some personal item of the one you love, or written request of your wish inside the pouch. For nine days you must repeat your desire three times each day. All the dolls had white and black pins attached to the cloth. The white pin was to wish someone well when it was pushed into the heart of the doll, whereas the black pin was pushed into the stomach to cause harm or pain.

Janelle found it all very amusing. She decided to buy the good fortune one for Harry the mailman, back in Crestview, who was always playing the lotto. Perhaps it would bring him luck.

She looked over all the smooth colorful stones that were in jars. Each color granted the wearer of the stone some magical power such as, healing, luck, or love. She put several stones in a basket to give out as small gifts to her staff, most were for good health and good fortune.

There were a collection of copper bracelets that were suppose to ward off arthritic pain and was in the process of selecting one for Mary, when she heard a voice say to her, "Congratulations, you've found love again haven't you?"

She turned to face the middle-aged round woman wearing a long white cotton dress with an attractive white hat trimmed with a red scarf. She wore a necklace made of black, brown and violet beads, intertwined with shells and teeth. There were silver rings on every finger and many bracelets, made out of twine... or maybe hair?

"Well is it true? Has love found you again?"

"Yes," Janelle whispered.

"I knew it, your aura is very bright, and you radiate an inner energy," said this amazing dark skinned Haitian woman with a thick lilting accent.

Angele approached them, "I see you've met my friend High Priestess Shabante."

"Yes I have and she is amazing. She just told me I have found love again."

"Why is that so amazing? I could have told you that, girl you're glowing. They all laughed, while Janelle's face and neck turned almost the same color as her red hair.

"Come," said Angele, "there is a table and chairs in the corner room where we can sit down and have a cup of tea. Do you like tea, Janelle?"

"Very much, I developed the habit while I lived in London."

"London? Look at this Angele, we have a traveler in our midst," said a laughing Shabante. "She is a daughter of the world. Who knows where she might settle next."

Angele served the tea, "Shabante is a very famous Priestess in Haiti. I have seen her do many wondrous things. Her powers are absolutely amazing. She is a very important spiritualist in the community especially during the Santeria drum and dance ceremonies. That's when she communicates with the serpent, but I'll never understand how she dances on fire without burning one inch of her body."

"Why you tell der dat? There is no fire in here. Dis pretty girl, she don need my help she has love surrounding her. Wait Janelle, let me hold your hand and take a good look at you." As Shabante studied Janelle, a frown came over her face as she said, "I would like to give you a reading. I have a feeling dat der is something you must know."

"I think it would be fun, I would love a reading."

"Would you like the Tarot Cards, a Palm reading or tea leaves."

"The tea leaves, yes, I choose the tea leaves," said a slightly cautious Janelle.

Angele heard the chimes, "Carry on without me," and left the room.

Shabante picked up a long decorative stick; which had a black chicken foot attached to the end. The handle had a painting of a snake coiled in the water around the earth. Above the claw was a rattle with many bones and long colorful ribbons. Shabante shook the staff over the table and then over Janelle's head as she started chanting."Ogun oinre o, welcome ogun of onire," as she waved the staff. "Now," she said as she put away the stick, and picked up a small cloth bag from her huge purse, "With dis bag of white sage, we will clean and purify dis space of negative spirits. You know, dey are all around us." She waved the pouch around the table and once again all around Janelle. "Dere now da air is pure."

Janelle only nodded feeling a little odd with all this ritual formality.

"We are now ready my dear, finish your tea. Good, now swirl de remaining liquid in da cup and very gently drain da rest onto your saucer. We must see where da leaves dey fall."

"Like this?"

"Yes dat's right now let me see. Oh my yes, you have had considerable sadness in your young life. I see you growing up alone and lonely. It has not been easy for you. You've always worked very hard. You did na mind the hard work when you found love. Dis was a happy time for a few years, den you parted. For a while your life was full yet empty. You see Janelle dat dis was a time for learning. It is wonderful dat you found him again; he is very good for you. Dis man is a worthy man dat has come back into your life. He is also very handsome, huh?"

"Yes very."

"You have been very successful in your efforts. I see you surrounded by people who love you. I think dis is because you are a good pers..." Just then her eyes glazed over as she slipped into a trance and started to chant while her huge body rocked back and forth.

Angele walked back into the room at the same time Shabante went into the trance. She put her fingers to her lips to warn Janelle not to talk. "Just listen," she whispered in Janelle's ear. "We mustn't break the spell."

"No need to look to the future!" She said in a strange deep man's voice. The air vibrated with the sound of the voice that was coming from Shabante's throat. "You must first look behind you for the answer," the voice hissed. "Ahead there is danger." Shabante's body shook back and forth so violently that she dropped the cup, which shattered as it hit the floor.

Angele ran to catch Shabante as her body swent into a spasm and she started to fall. The noise of the cup shattering woke her out of her trance. She looked dazed and confused as she rapidly blinked her eyes trying to focus.

Janelle poured her some tea, and held the cup to her mouth to help revive her. She sipped the tea, then grabbed Janelle's wrist and said, "Look behind you," this time in her own voice while looking very worried.

"I don't understand," said Janelle.

"Neither do I, it's something dat sometimes happens to me, I have no control over it. I will tell you dis very seriously Janelle, for I really like you, heed this warning and look behind you. Maybe in your past there was some unfinished business or some incident dat happened to you by a person dat is very evil."

"Don't worry, Janelle Etienne, Beau and I know many people. We will protect you," Angele said.

The ominous feeling within her suddenly changed her surrounding from fun to fear, as she stared at this woman. "I have a confession to make," she said as she rubbed her throbbing temples, "When my flight landed in New Orleans, I felt this overwhelming sense of fear. It was so strong that I couldn't move. My body became paralyzed.

"Ah, then it's true. Janelle don't you see you were being warned?" said Angele.

"What's this all about? I just don't understand why I would be in danger. I've never done anything to make someone want to hurt me. It's all so confusing."

"Janelle, I think I should call Beau and tell him to come and get you. I don't want you to be alone. You must take Shabante's warnings seriously."

"No, I'll be fine Angele," said Janelle as she rubbed her aching forehead, and then the back of her neck, only to discover goose bumps forming. "It's just a short walk to my hotel. I know Beau is tied up in an important meeting today, and I wouldn't want to bother him. Janelle saw a frown spread across Angele's face, and said, "don't worry its broad daylight, and it's only a few blocks."

"I'm sorry, even if you don't seriously heed the warnings, then I will! I'll call Etienne on his cell phone, but you will not leave my shop alone."

Shabante took Janelle's hand and said, "Sit daughter of the world, Shabante she gonna make a gris-gris for you."

"A what?"

"A gris-gris, there are many different kinds, this one is just for you." She reached into her bag, pulled out four jars, and placed them on the table. "For your gris-gris we need a pinch of chamomile for calming, a bay leaf for a clear mind, a touch of spearmint for healing and love, and a half teaspoon of dis powder."

"What kind of powder is that? Asked Janelle.

"Dis powder is the most important. It is part ground up chicken claw, part snake tail. It will protect you," said a very serious Shabante.

Janelle watched her mix all the ingredients together, and place them in a tiny glass vial. She then attached a long cord to the tiny vial and placed it around her neck.

"Now, you don have to worry no more, you are protected."

Janelle just nodded as tears welled up in her eyes. She just felt too drained to argue and surrendered her well being to her new friends.

Fifteen minutes later Etienne arrived at the shop, but this time he was not smiling. He took Janelle's hand, and said, "Angele told me everything. Now I know why you were the last one off the plane. Why didn't you tell me?"

"Oh Etienne, how could I? I felt so foolish!"

"Well you don't have to worry anymore. From now on you will be just fine. Come, I'll take you back to your hotel."

She thanked Shabante and Angele, paid for her purchases, and allowed Etienne to fuss over her. In the back of her mind she thought of the nightmares, and shuddered.

He took her back to her hotel, checked the room to make sure it was safe. He looked in every closet, under the bed, even in the shower.

"Etienne please, stop it. There is no one here it's safe. This is all probable nothing but superstition."

"Janelle, I've lived all my life in New Orleans. I have seen and heard things that I could never explain. Listen to your inner voice. What you felt when the plane landed was real. It's what some people refer to as intuition. The Chinese would say that your Chi has spoken; perhaps some would say your guardian angel is looking out for you. What ever you want to call it, you are being warned.

"Now, I'm going to give you my extra cell phone. Whenever you leave this room alone, I want you to always take it with you. I've programmed it with Beau's number, see, he is number one, and my number is two. In case we can't be reached, our friend, detective Dunbar Jones is three. You'll like Dunbar he is a really good guy. Now you promise me, don't leave this room ever without this phone. Ok?"

"Yes, thanks very much Etienne, I will."

"Now I'm going home to get dressed for the party tonight. If I'm even ten minutes late Angele will kill me," he laughed as he left the room.

She had been soaking in the tub for over forty minutes, ever since Etienne left. At the Voodoo shop, Angele had given her a gift of bath oil and the same fragrance candle and told her this is a wonderful way of relaxing. Aromatherapy's fragrance opens your mind, so that you could think clearly.' She was right, it was working as far as relaxing, but she was still confused as to who would want to hurt her.

She was startled when she heard a knocking at her door. She stood and reached for her terry bath- robe that she hurriedly wrapped around herself. "Just a minute," she shouted, as she covered her wet head with a towel, "I'll be right there."

She heard Beau's frantic voice calling her, "Janelle are you all right?"

She opened the door to see Beau looking very worried. He rushed in and took her in his arms. "Oh God," he exclaimed, "I was so worried when Etienne called me and told me what had happened, but now that you're in my arms I know everything will be fine. I just can't lose you Janelle. I've waited so long for you."

His words felt so reassuring. How could anything possibly happen to her when she was wrapped in his love? "I'm fine Beau really, it's all just so silly. Come sit down, I'll pour you a drink." She had ordered a bottle of wine when she came back to the hotel. She thought she and Beau would have a glass of wine before leaving for the ball.

"God you're beautiful, even with your hair wrapped in a towel. I guess I interrupted your bath," said Beau. "It's too bad I didn't arrive sooner, I could have joined you," he said as he kissed her.

"Why it's not too late at all. As a matter of fact I was just going to run some fresh water so you just might as well join me."

She ran the water and added the oil that Angele had given her. The fragrance that filled the air did feel very relaxing, or was it just the presence of Beau beside her.

As they soaked in the tub, his arms around her, she wondered if two people could ever feel as close as they did at this moment. Perhaps it was the flickering light of the candle, the soothing music of Mozart's piano concerto playing on the radio, or was it the aromatherapy? Whatever it was it was working. She felt safe and loved; what more could anyone want out of life.

"Tell me about your meetings," she said as she snuggled closer to him.

"To tell you the truth, Janelle, I found it very difficult to concentrate on the business at hand. My thoughts kept drifting to you and what a wonderful time we had last night."

"I know what you mean Beau. Angele and Shabante were commenting at how I was glowing with love. I guess it show, and I'm proud of it," she said with delight.

"I'm worried about you Janelle. I think you should be very careful."

"Beau, like I told you, it's just superstition; besides Shabante made this gris-gris for me, see," as she held up the small vile.

"Good, I know all of this must sound silly to someone who didn't grow up in these surroundings," his eyes squinted as he shook his head, but Janelle, there are some people who truly do have the power to see into the future and to warn you of an impending event that might harm you. I don't know whether it's valid or not, I just know there are mysteries that I cannot pretend to understand, nor ignore. From now on you must be careful."

"Ok. I won't argue with you," she sighed rather pensively. She stood and pulled him to his feet. He wrapped a towel around her, kissing her neck, as he slowly turned her around and once again their bodies melted into each other.

The Toad

Mala parked the Jaguar in a no parking zone on Decatur Street. She didn't care, it was only a car, and her father would take care of it. That's all he's good for, and I'm in a hurry, she thought. I'll show him! I too can take care of people who get in my way; after all I am my father's daughter.

She walked aimlessly, her mind, full of hatred oblivious to her surroundings, as she pushed people out of her way. She didn't realize or care that she was talking aloud and attracting attention from people who passed by. She crossed the street against the light, cars honked, tires squealed as they swerved to miss her.

"I'm just as clever as him," she said while wildly waving her hands in the air. "Let's see how will I do this? I got my way with Beau before by putting a drug in his drink, but I don't think I could get close enough to Janelle to poison her."

"Why didn't he ever buy me a gun when I asked him to?" she said to a derelict who was drinking in a doorway. "See I'm right he never gave me anything. Terrible Tyler, huh! What a joke!"

The derelict looked up at her with glazed eyes and laughed, "yeah Missy what a joke!" He looked around and said, "This is all a big joke," as he waved his bottle in the air.

Mala didn't notice the tough looking young man who

135

stood deep in the shadow of the doorway, dressed in dirty jeans and a torn green shirt. However, he looked very interested in her, especially when he heard her mention the gun and Terrible Tyler's name.

Mala glared at the derelict, wrinkled her nose and walked away in disgust.

She entered into the French Market, as the vendors were just setting up their stalls for the weekend. In her haste she bumped into a table that one of the Korean families had set up full of wallets, and various eel skin items.

"Damn it," she yelled, "Get that crap out of my way," as she pushed over the table.

The family, yelled at her in their native tongue, as they scramble to protect their only way of making a living in this new land.

As she walked, she remembered overhearing a phone conversation of her father's. He had arranged to get rid of someone who was in his way. Although, when she confronted him he only denied it with such an innocent looking face. What a liar he was, he could have helped her, he could have arranged for someone to kill that bitch Janelle. He always told her that as long as you have money you could arrange for other people to do your dirty work, this way your hands don't get soiled. Well, I'll do it. I'll pay someone to get rid of her I have lots of money.

I heard him mention a place. I know it's near the French Market, let me think Lennys? No that not the name; was it, Lonny's End? No, "think Mala,"

"I got it! There it is," she squinting at the sign..."The Lion's Den." It was a small bar tucked away on a side street about a block away, but she could see the sign with the picture of a lion. She quickly walked toward the small bar, smiling very pleased with herself on having found the answer to her problem.

She'd show her father just how easy it was to get rid of someone. She smiled, and thought, it's funny what you learn from your parents.

In her quest to hire someone, she didn't realize that the man in the torn green shirt, and the dead eyes was following her.

She boldly entered the bar and was temporarily blinded by its darkness. As her eyes adjusted she noticed how dirty it was. A splattering of customers, leaned against the worn out counter, not exactly the upper class of society that she was so accustomed to.

She headed for the empty stools at the end of the bar, so she I could have a private conversation with the bartender.

"What'll it be lady?"

"Give me a glass of Cabernet Savignon."

"You lost or something, look around you, this ain't the Ritz! I'll give you a glass of red wine."

She sat sipping the cheap bitter wine, and tried to figure out what to do next, when a man came and sat next to her. She noticed how grungy he looked.

He leaned over and whispered, "Lady, buy me a drink and I'll tell yah whatcha wanna know."

She was repulsed at the sight of this dirty smiling man, with missing front teeth, and tattered clothes.

"And what do you think I want to know?"

"You wanna know bout guns right? I can tell; why else wud a babe like you be sittin in a place like this? Now if you're gonna buy that drink make it a double whiskey no ice."

Now he had Mala's complete attention. "Bartender, give my friend here a double whiskey, no ice." She waited a minute and then whispered viciously, "Well get on with it! Where do I buy a gun?"

The bartender rolled his eyes as if to say now I've seen it all, as he set down the drink and scooped up Mala's money.

The dirty man picked up his drink with two hands to keep if from spilling, and drained the whiskey in one gulp. Even in the darkness Mala couldn't help noticing his dirty half-bitten nails.

"That depends," said the stranger now fortified with the whiskey. "Do you wanna a gun clean, never bin used? You see that's more money, like seven or eight bills. A dirty one is a lot cheaper," he explained as he noticed her confusion. "Look, you know it's not like it's dirty, it was only used once, but that one I could get in a hurry. No questions asked, no registration."

"I'll take the used one, I don't care, and I want it now, I just want her dead!"

"Shh! Not so loud, calm down. Let me asks you, do you wanna do it yourself?"

"Why?" Mala's eyes narrowed suspiciously.

"Well lady for a thousand more you don't have to get yur pretty hands dirty, if you know what I mean."

She took another sip of wine, and was surprised at how good it was starting to taste. "Who will do it, you?"

"Don't worry it's easy to get rid of someone. Ah, I don't know you, and you don't know me, see? No ties, now that's what counts, no ties. Give me the money, and I'll do it for yah. Just tell me who youse wants dun in and where dey lives."

Mala reached over to the newspaper at the end of the bar. She tore out the picture of Beau and Janelle on the front page and handed it to him.

"That's her! She's staying at the Maison de Ville Hotel. It seems the little tramp made something of her-self, and is being honored with some sort of stupid trophy."

He looked at the picture, folded it up and slid it into his pocket. "I'll take care of it," he said as he held out his hand palm up, "now gimme the bread."

"What?"

"The money, gimme the two grand and she'll be dead by tomorrow night.

"Why so long? Why not right now? Hey, wait a minute! I thought you said it would be around sixteen hundred, now it's two thousand?"

"Lady, listen it's not that easy. I said about eighteen C's. I have to hook up with people and get the gun." He frowned, scratched his head and said, "Then I gotta look for the right time, yuh know? I'm really sticking my neck out. It's two grand or I walk."

"All right I hear you. I just want you to know I'm not stupid. You're a complete stranger, and how do I know you're not just going to take my money and disappear?"

"Ok, listen we just got's to trust each other, ya know," drumming his fingers on the bar while he thinks. "Let's see now...why don't you give me half now and half when the job is done, and lady, don't cross me cuz if I snuff her, and you don't pay me, I'll do you. You can count on it!" He looked at her, and she sucked in her breath when she looked into his black cold dead eyes.

"I'll pay you. I want her out of my life, and out of my way. "She picked up her purse and started pulling out her cosmetic bag, house keys and a few other incidentals, searching for her money.

"Please lady, take it slow, pass the money to me so no one sees," he whispered.

"I only have eight hundred with me. I'll give you the rest tomorrow when it's all over, I promise. Ok?"

"I guess it's all right, but not here. I'll meet you at Crazy

Sally's Bar on Bourbon Street, around midnight. You know where it's at?"

"Yes it's a deal, she said as she slipped off the stool. Desperate to get away from the disgusting dirty man she quickly walked out the door into the bright sunlight.

The Trophy

Janelle was happy, though slightly nervous, as she dressed for her party. She was uncertain of the dress she bought on Rodeo Drive. And hoped it wasn't too plain. The simple long black strapless crepe dress; showed off her small waist and slim hips. It had a trim of tiny black beads across the low cut top that revealed a hint of fullness and a touch of cleavage. The sheer chiffon shawl also is trimmed with a row of black beads.

Her curly red hair was swooped up, and held in place by a large black onyx antique comb, given to her by the Countess de Marie in Spain. She had said it would help create an elegant coiffure, and it did. Her long teardrop earrings and necklace were black onyx surrounded by diamond chips. She remembered fondly the day she and Lizzie had found them in a little antique shop around the corner from the Louve in Paris.

So many memories of happy but empty times, empty because she was without Beau in her life. She made a mental note to call Lizzie and Percy. She missed them and wanted them to know about her trophy and of course, Beau.

The earrings and the necklace were perfect with the dress. She applied the last touch, just a drop of perfume, behind her ears and in her cleavage, when she heard Beau calling her name as he knocked at the door. She hurriedly glanced in the mirror one last time, checking every detail. She did want to look nice, but just for him, so he would be proud of her.

As she opened the door to greet him, she heard him suck in his breath. "Janelle," he exclaimed, "You're absolutely stunning! I'm not sure I want to leave this room with you looking like that. I wouldn't want anyone to steal you away from me."

Janelle blushed, looked up at his handsome face and said…"Beau, I could never leave you now. You've captured my heart, you must know that."

"Come," he said as he took her hand, "there are over three hundred people downstairs, waiting to honor you."

When they walked into the Mardi Gras Ball room, they were met with a standing ovation for Janelle. Flashbulbs popped, as the band played, 'California Here I Come.'

Mr. Thodus stepped up to the podium with Janelle, and motioned for the guests and the photographers to quiet down. Within a few minutes a hush fell over the room.

"Thank you all for attending this gala affair," he said with a slight quiver in his voice. "I'm going to make this speech short and sweet, because I know how hungry you all are." When everyone laughed and applauded, Janelle could see Mr. Thodus start to physically relax. His voice became a little steadier, his head held a little higher as his confidence rose.

"As you all know," he continued, "We are honoring Janelle Connors, from the Sand Box Restaurant in Crestview California. She has come to our attention because of her exceptional cuisine, which we will all be experiencing to-night." The crowd applauded as he smiled and motioned for silence. "There are copies at each table of her Apricot

Pork Chop recipe with couscous, and for dessert Sicilian Ricotta Torte, for your continued enjoyment." He looked down at his notes, adjusted his glasses, looked up and sincerely said, "I hope you all have a wonderful time tonight. Now it gives me great pleasure to present this trophy from the New Orleans Twenty First Greatest Chefs Convention, to Ms Janelle Connors!"

The applause was deafening to her ears, and she wondered what she had done to deserve so many people honoring her." Thank you all so very much," she said as she accepted the trophy. "I'm overwhelmed by your support." Tiny tears of happiness were starting to well up in her eyes, she swallowed hard as she nervously said; "I will always treasure this moment, for now I know the true meaning of Southern Hospitality. You are all so gracious, and from the bottom of my heart, I thank each and everyone again," as she held up her trophy and walked down the steps to Beau.

"You did great," he said as he took her into his arms and kissed her. He stepped back and said, "I'm so very proud of you." Beau took her by the arm to guide her. "Come, I want you to meet my parents, of course you know they already love you. He escorted her to the table, where a handsome middle-aged couple sat.

"Janelle, this is my father Jonn and my mother Rachel. Mom and dad this is Janelle, the woman that has a tight hold on my heart."

Jonn and Rachel made such a fuss over Janelle, that she immediately felt like she had known them all her life. During dinner they discussed her travels and her restaurant. By the time desert was served, Janelle adored Beau's parents.

After dinner the band began to play and Beau asked her to dance. He held her close as their bodies swayed to the music. She whispered in his ear, "please don't let the music stop, I love being in your arms."

He smiled and said, "Sweetheart it seems I have loved you forever. I could never go back to living without you. Please marry me. I promise I will do everything in my power to make you happy. Say yes darling, please say yes."

Janelle stopped dancing, she looked at him with tears streaming down her face and said, "Oh yes Beau, a thousand times yes, how could it possibly be any other way. I too have to be with you, and I promise I will do everything within my power to make you happy."

He took her into his arms and in the middle of the dance floor, they kissed as a crowd formed around them applauding, He stopped kissing her and held her hand up high and shouted to everyone, "We're engaged!" They all congratulated them as they walked back to tell his parents.

Beau's father kissed her and said; "I always thought my son was smart, now I am certain of it."

Janelle's eyes were brimming with tears again, as she whispered to them, "I'm so fortunate to have found someone as loving as your son, and I would just love to be part of your wonderful family.

Rachel looked at Janelle and at her son, who were so full of joy, nodded to her husband, and slipped her magnificent diamond ring from her finger. She took her son's hand and put her ring in his palm. She turned to Janelle and said with tears of joy, "I always wondered who my son would choose for a wife. If I could have chosen for him, I definitely would have selected you. This ring has been in our family for generations, and now I would be proud to have my son present it to you."

As Beau put the ring on Janelle's finger the photographers went wild with pictures and questions.

"That's enough," said Jonn. "This is a time for celebrating! Waiter bring us your finest champagne, while I dance with my soon to be daughter in law, if it's all right with you son?"

"Beau beamed as he took his mother's hand and let her to the dance floor he said, "We'll I'll just dance with your charming wife."

As Janelle danced, she silently thanked the heavens for the most fantastic night of her life. I promise you Lord that the two of us together will work hard to right some of the wrongs of this earth.

Mala's father sat at a table close by, observing the festivities. He drummed his fingers nervously with one hand while rubbing his aching eyes with the other. He worried about Mala. His private detectives scoured the French Quarter looking for her, so far nothing. Not a sign. A well-dressed man holding an envelope tapped him on the shoulder, bent down whispered in his ear. Tyler Monroe motioned him to sit down and had the waiter bring him a drink. He sighed, straightened his shoulders and with shaking hands, he opened the envelope.

It was a report on Mala from the detectives. Her car was found on Canal St. A Korean family had watched her go into a bar called the Lions Den. She was last seen in the presence of a drug addict whom everyone calls the Toad, he is a real low life from the ghetto with a long criminal record.

Tyler was upset over the report, and thought it couldn't get much worse, when the detective leaned over and whispered, "Mr. Tyler, it doesn't look good. She was seen at the Lions Den giving the Toad money. I had to pay the bartender off to keep him quiet."

Tyler stood up, shook hands with the detective. "Thanks so much for coming to tell me in person. You can expect a healthy bonus for your excellent work."

The detective patted him on the back and said, "I'm really very sorry Mr. Tyler for all your troubles, I'm sure we'll find her soon," and left the room.

Tyler sat at his table and wondered where he had failed. How had his life become so messed up? Everything he had given so much importance to now seem worthless. He had always assumed if he were rich and powerful he could buy or control everything. Right, he thought, everything but happiness. All the dirty dealings, all the cheating to attain more and more money only brought him misery.

The only course open to me, he thought, is to make things right. He rose with great determination and walked over to Beau.

Out of the corner of his eye, Beau saw the big man walking toward him. He knew instinctively that this was trouble.

"Congratulations Beau," Tyler said as he shook Beau's hand, his head was down eyes looking at the floor as he cleared his throat. "I wish you happiness."

Beau had difficulty responding, he was so surprised at Tyler's appearance. He could only nod his head.

"I know this is a bad time, but I must speak to you privately. I have something very important to discuss with you."

Beau looked closely at the big mans face, and was shocked. It was obvious that Tyler the Terrible had been crying. He took the man's arm, walked to the corner of the room and said, "Tell me what is this very important news?"

"It's Mala," he said as his shoulders sagged.

It seemed to Beau that Tyler's whole demeanor had changed. This man, who Beau always thought was a man of power and strength, was after all human.

"She saw the picture of you and Janelle in the paper, and has gone crazy. I tried to calm her down, I wanted to leave town with her. Perhaps take her someplace where she could get some help. I tried, I really did," he sobbed.

"What happened?" he asked as he felt his heart drop to his stomach.

"She wants, oh how do I explain this?" he straightens his shoulders and blurts the words out with great force. "She wants Janelle dead!"

"Oh my God, then it's true. She was being warned of something from the past. Shabante was right."

"Shabante, someone else knows? Who is Shabante?"

"Never mind, tell me what else you know."

"I just received a report from one of the detectives I had hired to find Mala. She has been missing since early this morning. He told me that she was last seen paying a low life druggy a large sum of money."

"She is buying drugs again?"

"Again, what do you mean again?"

"That all happened a long time ago, it doesn't matter now."

"I'm afraid Beau that it wasn't drugs, she bought. I think she hired a hit man. When she left the house in a rage this morning, it was to buy a gun, not drugs. Like I said she wants to have Janelle killed."

Beau turned white, as his mind raced with ways to protect Janelle. "Mr. Monroe," he said as he sincerely shook his hand, "I know this must have been the most difficult thing you have ever faced in your life, and I really appreciate your confiding in me. Right now I have to make a few phone calls. Hopefully all of this can be resolved without anyone getting hurt."

"Thanks Beau, I pray it's so," as Tyler the Terrible, now a broken man, turned and walked out of the room with shoulders sagging and head down.

Beau glanced over at Janelle to make sure she was all right as he reached into his pocket for his cell phone. Nothing must happen to her. He dialed Dunbar Jones number and anxiously prayed he would answer. On the third ring he heard his familiar voice. Beau exhaled with a sigh of relief and said, "Dunbar, it's Beau, I need you. It's very important that we meet for breakfast, say about eight tomorrow morning?"

"Sure Beau what's up?"

"I'll explain everything tomorrow at the Hotel Maison de Ville coffee shop. Thanks Dunbar, you're the best." As he put the phone into his jacket pocket, he silently prayed for help.

Apricot Pork Chops
(Serves Four)

8 medium to thin pork chops
2 large sweet onions sliced very thin
4 tbsp. of apricot preserve
1 tbsp. of Olive Oil

Fry pork chops in one tablespoon of olive oil until brown on both sides. Remove from frying pan and add sliced onions. Cook until onions are sautéed. Add four tablespoons of Apricot Preserve to onions and cook for about three minutes until onions are slightly caramelized. Add pork chops back to frying pan until preserve and onions coat the chops. Salt and pepper to taste. Serve immediately with a serving of couscous and blanched string beans with a light balsamic vinegarette dressing. Sprinkle cold string beans with slivered almonds.

Couscous

2/3 Cup of dry couscous (Moroccan pasta)
$\frac{1}{2}$ cup of chopped dried apricots
$\frac{1}{4}$ cup of toasted pine nuts

In medium saucepan, combine 2-1/2 cups water, 4 teaspoons olive oil or butter and $\frac{1}{2}$ cup of chopped dried apricots. Bring to a boil. Stir in couscous. Cover, and remove from heat. Let stand five minutes. Fluff couscous lightly with a fork before serving. Makes five cups.

Sicilian Ricotta Torte

1 pound cake, about 9"x3"
1 tbsp. Grand Marnier or Orange liquor
1 lb. Ricotta cheese (2 cups), drained
2/3 cup finely chopped toasted almonds
1/3 cup superfine sugar
2 tbsp. whipping cream
1 tsp. vanilla extract
3 oz. miniature semisweet chocolate

Using a serrated knife cut pound cake horizontally into $\frac{1}{2}$ inch thick slices; set aside, taking care not to break them. Place cheese, sugar and whipping cream in a food processor fitted with a steel blade. Process until smooth, 1 minute. Add vanilla, and liqueur; process just to blend. Place cheese mixture in a medium bowl; fold in almonds and chocolate pieces. Spread slice with cheese mixture; add a second cake slice. Check that slices are perfectly aligned atop of each other and none of filling oozes out between layers. Refrigerate cake while preparing Chocolate Glaze.

Chocolate Glaze

$\frac{1}{2}$ pint whipping cream (1 cup)
1 tbsp. Grand Marnier or Orange liquor
8 oz. semisweet chocolate, chopped

To prepare Chocolate Glaze; in a heavy 2 qt. Saucepan over medium-low heat, combine cream and chocolate. Cook, stirring, until chocolate melts and mixture is smooth and uniform in color. Remove from heat; stir in liqueur.

Place cake on a serving platter. Drizzle chocolate mixture over cake, always working from top to completely coat. Refrigerate until ready to serve. Makes 10 to 12 servings

Dunbar Jones

Dunbar Jones sat waiting for his friend Beau in the coffee shop, doing his all time favorite thing, studying people while sipping his coffee au laite, and munching on powdered sugared beignets. Occasionally he would jot down a few sentences in his ever-present notebook. His kind moon shape face, and his bright smile against his dark chocolate colored skin, made most people take to him. When he smiled you felt the room light up.

Dunbar had been through it all and survived, largely because of his humor. Anytime, anything had gone wrong, he'd laugh at it all first and then find a way to solve the problem.

His life had always been hard, since his childhood. Although he tried so many times not to think about it every now and then, the memory of it all comes back, to haunt him and it seems like yesterday.

He was just ten years old when it happened. It was the day of the Baptist Church picnic. He could still see the happy faces of his parents and brothers. He liked going to church, it was fun, especially when the music started. Oh how he loved the music. He would clap his hands while his whole body swayed back and forth, and even if he wanted to, he couldn't keep his feet from dancing.

"When Moses stood on holy ground he knew what had to be," Minister Brown's strong, deep baritone voice sang out. "He went straight to the Pharaoh and said set my people free."

His Auntie Evie was in the choir, wearing her long gold and purple robe. She looked like she sang only to him, as she danced and twirled to the music. He clapped his hands, threw up his arms, and shouted with the rest of the congregation. "Come on and leave. You've got to leave it in the hands of the lord. Leave your burden leave your heart-ache leave it all in the hands of the lord," he cried out, while his whole body vibrated to the wonderful sound that filled the small church.

It was a different story during the sermon; Dunbar was fidgety and anxious for the sermon to end because now all he could think of was food. The wonderful food he soon would be eating. He knew there would be barbequed chicken and ribs, the gumbo he always loved, and his very favorite sweet potatoes with pecans.

"Well are you hungry boy?" his father asked him. "Cause it's time to eat, or are you just goanna sit in church all day?"

He smiled and thought, even after all these years, he could still remember how he was up and out of the church so fast it made his entire family laugh, because it was no secret that Dunbar was always hungry.

That was the best and the worst day of his life. He ate his fill, until he thought he would burst. He played games with the other kids and chased the girls, until his mother begged him to stop. He remembered, as a lump filled his throat and he blinked to hold back the tears, that she was scolding him...when it happened.

Out of the corner of his eye he saw their neighbor

Samuel, a very large violent man when drunk, pushed his father. His father pushed Samuel back and a fight ensued. He ran over to help his dad, when he saw Samuel pick up a bottle and smash it across his father's forehead. Blood splattered everywhere, as his father fell to the ground

Dunbar hit Samuel as hard as he could yelling at him to leave his father alone, when Samuel picked little Dunbar up by his ears, and in his drunken rage he savagely threw him against the tree. Dunbar slumped down to the ground like a broken doll and lay there until his Auntie Evie ran to help him. She picked him up, checked him for broken bones, all the while sobbing and hugging him. Everyone around him was crying and screaming. His mother had run to his father's side and he could see she was shouting but he couldn't hear anything. He just stood there, in his now silent world staring at his father's bloody body.

They buried his dad two days later. After the funeral his Auntie Evie noticed that something was wrong with Dunbar. His eyes were glazed, and he hadn't spoken to anyone since the picnic.

The next day she took him to a doctor, in her heart she knew what he was going to say. The doctor examined Dunbar; he checked his eyes and his ears, sighed and sadly shook his head. He told Auntie Evie that Dunbar was just starting to come out of shock, but unfortunately the ears were seriously damaged. She cried when he told her that Dunbar was deaf.

Things at home changed drastically after his father died. They had been poor before, barely getting by, but now they were down right destitute. There were many times when they ate a full meal, only once a week. Most of the time, it was just watered down soup and bread.

He now lived in a very silent world and out of his

loneliness he turned to books. His favorites as a child were Tom Sawyer, and Huckleberry Finn. He just couldn't read enough about all their adventures, and laughed at all the trouble they got themselves into.

Dunbar was suddenly becoming aware of his surroundings. For the first time in his young life, he noticed how really white the clouds looked against the blue sky. The leaves on the trees he thought at one time were just plain green, but now he could see several different shades of green, a little yellow and yes, even some red and orange.

Although he had lost his hearing, all his other senses were sharpened. He could smell cigarette and pipe smoke from five blocks away. At night from his bedroom window he was overpowered by the sweet scent of the night blooming Jasmine. It's funny, he thought, he never noticed the aroma before.

The only thing he truly missed was the music he so loved. In his silent world he kept repeating the last song he had heard, and he would sing it to himself, "Leave your burden, leave your heart ache, come on and leave it in the hands of the Lord."

He began to turn to other wonders to combat his loneliness, like observing various animals. He especially liked the chipmunks. He would sit quietly for hours by the stream and count the many times that the little creatures would scurry back and forth looking for acorns for their den. When he couldn't find a chipmunk, he would study the ants. They always looked so busy, like they were part of a big family all working together.

Within a year, Dunbar had graduated to studying people. He could tell how they felt by the way they carried themselves. Shoulders back with head held high meant they were sure of themselves and in control. Folded arms across their chest, was an indication that they were protecting themselves. He noticed that when people were embarrassed their hands would cover part of the face while the eyes looked down. He could tell if someone was nervous, for they would tug on their ear, or keep brushing invisible lint from their clothes. If a person were agitated the fist would open and close continuously.

He chuckled to himself as he remembered that he had read that the ancient orator Cicero had said, 'everything is in the face,' and it was true. Dunbar started to notice little things, like a lifted brow meant they were puzzled, or questioning a point. Happiness, boredom, anger, sadness, embarrassment, indifference, and utter devastation, would all be written on one's face.

Many people are judged by the words they speak, but after Dunbar learned how to read faces, he knew that words quite often were untrue. He could always spot a liar. It would show right there in the eyes, like a phony politician who sought a vote. The lips would part in a bright smile, but the eyes are full of indifference. So many sales clerks would say, "Have a nice day," and smile, but the smile never reached the eyes. He would always focus on the eyes, they told the truth.

He remembered a conversation he had had with an acquaintance that told him he could always lie to his girl friends with a straight face, and they would never know the difference. Dunbar hated to burst his bubble, but when this man lied his eyes opened wider, his expression seemed to freeze and his eyes had a blank look to them, like that of a doll's. Studying people was all very interesting and kept Dunbar much too busy to ever feel sorry for himself.

When he was thirteen they moved to the Bayou, where his mother had gotten a job cleaning crawfish. He liked the swamps; there was always food there, if you knew where to look for it.

His neighbors were a mixture of Cajun, Choctaw Indians, and ancestors of runaway slaves, known as Maroons. It was the Choctaw Indians who had protected the Maroons by hiding them deep in the swamps from the slave traders. One of his best friends was half Choctaw and half Maroon, he was very knowledgeable about the swamps and taught him how to hunt Indian style; to walk without frightening off the many deer, frogs, alligators, and other animals hiding in the dark murky waters of the swamps.

Dunbar was well liked by his neighbors, especially Louie. He was a proud Cajun, descendant of a 17th century French colonist from the shore of Canada's, Bay Acadia.

Louie taught Dunbar how to catch the catfish that scavenged along the bottom of shallow water. He also showed Dunbar how to maneuver the boat through the thick carpet of duckweed that covered the water with tiny green flowers, while hiding the fish and the long green snakes that slithered across the weeds.

The swamps were amazing, sometimes frightening, yet other times beautiful. When they were out in the boat Louie would signal to Dunbar to be careful of the alligators that were languishing in the sun one minute, while slithering from dry land to green dirty looking water the next. Or the scene would turn into a sight to behold. Dunbar's favorite was riding through the swamps, from murky water to suddenly as far as the eye could see, he would come across the beauty of the bayou clogged with light purple water Hyacinths turning the scene from scary to beautiful.

Louie showed Dunbar everything about the swamps. He taught him how to catch ducks for supper, and to watch out for the marsh hawks. He educated him on where to find the swamp rabbits, the river otters, and night herons and how to catch the white nutria's and sell them for their fur.

Dunbar loved visiting Louie and his clan. The Cajun are wonderful down to earth people that love life. They live in crude shacks, very seldom wear shoes, never put on airs, and believe in living the good life.

Louie wasn't much of a talker, that's one of the reason he liked Dunbar, he didn't have to talk to a deaf kid. Dunbar learned everything about the bayou by watching Louie. It was very fascinating to watch him skin an alligator, and cook the flesh Cajun style; his favorite was Alligator Etouffee. After they ate their fill of Louie's wonderful spicy cooking he would take Dunbar to the Trading Post and sell the alligator hide for quite a bit of money, which the two of them would split. The extra money came in handy for his mom. Every time Louie paid Dunbar he would write him a note of profound sayings, one in particular was, "Remember son, money it don't buy time, so enjoy your life as the good lord gives it to you. Dieu te beni."

Yeah, Dunbar was sure happy in the bayou. He wasn't hungry any more; he could always find something to eat in the swamps. He even liked the fog shrouded mornings, with the strong mixed smell of dogwood blossoms, wild azalea and pine trees. The only thing he truly missed was the sound of music.

One day he was sitting on the dock of the Trading Post fishing with his younger brother Benny. It was one of those lazy summer days when everything seemed right, and for some unknown reason he felt awfully lucky. Dunbar turned around for the bait can, when he saw a young woman struggling to tie her boat to the dock. He put his fishing rod down and ran to help the woman secure the boat.

"Thanks," she said, "That was very nice of you to help me. Come on, I'll buy you a soda."

"He can't hear you miss," said Benny. He's gone deaf when big Sam hit him in the head."

Now this was truly a very fortuitous day for Dunbar, because this young lady Ms Rana, was a teacher who had come back to the Bayou to take care of her invalid mother. She had just left a position where she was teaching deaf children sign language and how to read lips. Yes indeed, Dunbar remembers, now that was a lucky day, almost as if she was sent to the bayou just for him.

He quickly learned the art of sign language, but reading lips was his all time favorite. He was overjoyed, because now he could communicate with everyone. When combining his knowledge of observation and his skill at lip reading. Dunbar was extremely good at understanding the human race.

After he had graduated from high school, Dunbar got a job with the oil people on the banks of the bayou. One day he stayed late and helped his boss fix a broken part on one of the main rigs. After it was fixed they went for a drink at The Trading Post, and they got discussing what had happened to cause Dunbar's loss of hearing.

His boss took out a business card, handed it to Dunbar and said, "Look kid, my son is a doctor, and he's damn good. I'm giving you the day off tomorrow and I want you to go see him. Tell him I sent you, he'll take care of you, and it's on me."

Now, as he remembers that day, his face lights up as he smiles, for it was really a miracle for him. After taking x-rays it was discovered that all he needed was a very simple operation that was performed right there and then in the doctor's office, and lo and behold he could hear again.

He was now nineteen years old, and had been deaf for almost ten years to the day. It was amazing; he had walked in living in a silent world, and walked out hearing all the noises of life that everyone takes for granted. The first thing he did was go to church to say thanks to God and to listen to the wonderful music.

It took him a ling time before he got used to the noises of the bayou especially at night when he was trying to fall asleep. He could hear the rustling of the leaves on the trees even if there was only a slight breeze. The croaking of the frogs calling to each other, the chirping of the crickets, the cry of a wounded bird, and the loud noise of the water lapping against the dock were deafening. The noises of the night kept him awake for hours, until he gave up and stuffed cotton in his ears. Once again, his world was turned upside down, this time for the better, because now he could hear the music he so loved.

He had to give up his job because the noise of the oil pumps gave him headaches. That probably was a blessing in disguise, because with his knowledge of people, and his ability to read lips, he became the best detective on the New Orleans force.

Dunbar looked at his watch, and thought Beau should be here any minute now. He stirred his coffee, picked up the cup and took a sip. His eyes scanned the room, and old habits took over as he started to read the lips of the middle aged man and the tearful young girl across the room. He chuckled and thought oh yeah, give it to him good girl, that old coot deserves it. He was so engrossed in reading their lips that he didn't even notice Beau as he approached the table.

"Caught you again huh Dunbar/ I think I'm going to have to pass a law that will prohibit you from eavesdropping on people's conversation with your eyes. Yeah, that's it. I should call my secretary and get started on it right now!"

Dunbar stood up as he and Beau hugged and patted each other on the back like old friends do.

"Beau, please hold off on that law until I finish

eavesdropping, this is just starting to get good. You see that old coot over there? Well he's been lying to that pretty young girl. He told her his marriage was over, and that his wife and he were living apart for the last two years. Now that she is pregnant he is telling her that he has to go back to his very sick wife or she is going to have a mental breakdown, and he would feel very guilty if she shot herself and died.

"Do women really fall for that old line?"

"Wait, that's not all. Now this is really getting good, she just told him that when she went to the ladies room fifteen minutes ago she called his wife and asked her to join them so they could all sit down and discuss a divorce.

"That's why he stood up so abruptly. He almost spilled the water that was sitting on the table," he laughed.

"Well here's the good part," said Dunbar, "I would be willing to bet you that the woman standing in the doorway looking around the room is his wife."

"How can you tell?" asked Beau.

"Look at how she is standing, like she is ready to do battle. See her clenched fist, her furrow brow, and her eyes, man they are angry."

"Yes, your right again," said Beau as they both watched her walk with great determination to the table and smack her husband across the face with her purse.

"I swear Dunbar, you've got the gift. That's why I have to impose upon you for your help. I'm really worried, and I have this gut feeling that only you could make things right."

Dunbar frowned, as he looked at beau's face. Caesar was right he could see how frightened Beau was by the look in his eyes; like a trapped animal crying for help. The smile left Dunbar's face as he became very serious; he picked up his pen and reached for his notebook. "Of course Beau, you know I'm ready to help anytime, anywhere. Tell me what's going on."

Alligator Etouffee

1 lb alligator meat (or chicken) cut in thin strips
½ cup green onions, chopped

2 onions chopped   2 sticks butter
4 stalks chopped celery   ¼ cup minced parsley
Salt, cayenne and black   2 cloves garlic, minced
    pepper   1-can tomatoes

Sauté onions, garlic and celery in butter until soft. Add tomatoes and simmer for 20 minutes in covered iron pot. Add alligator meat and allow to cook over low heat until tender about 1 hour. If gravy is too thick add a little hot water. Serve over hot rice.

Gumbo

1-1/2 lbs. Okra   2 lbs peeled shrimp
1 pt. oysters   1 lb crabmeat
Parsley   Green onions

Cut okra in small pieces. Simmer slowly in 2 tbs. oil, stirring often to prevent scorching. Add to basic sauce and continue cooking for 20 minutes. Add shrimp and crab neat, cook 10 minutes and then add oysters. Add enough water or seafood stock to give the sauce the consistency of thick soup. Cook another 20 minutes after the mixture begins to boil. About 10 minutes before serving, add the onions and parsley. Serve in soup bowls with rice. A little garlic bread goes well with gumbo. Cut up chicken and smoked sausage may be used if seafood is not available.

Mashed Sweet Potatoes
(With Louisiana Pecans)

3 lbs of yams or sweet potatoes
$\frac{1}{4}$ cup unsalted butter room temperature, cut into pieces
1-1/2 tbs. brown sugar
1 tsp. grated lemon peel
1 tsp. grated orange peel
1 egg beaten to blend
1 cup coarsely chopped pecans

Place yams on baking sheet in 350o oven. Pierce with fork. Roast until tender, about one hour 15 minutes. Cool slightly. Peel yams, transfer to bowl and mash. Stir in butter, sugar, lemon and orange peel, while yams are still hot, mix egg into yam mixture, transfer to baking dish. Sprinkle pecans over. Bake in 350o oven until heated through, about one hour. Serves four.

Beignets

1 cup of water
1 cup of milk
1 egg beaten
3 cups of flour
2 tbs. of baking powder

1 tsp. salt
2 tsp. sugar
Oil for frying
Confectioners' sugar

Mix water, milk and eggs; add flour, baking powder, salt, and 2 teaspoons of sugar and mix until smooth.

Drop by spoonfuls into 2 inches of hot oil at 375 degrees; drain on paper towels and sprinkle with confectioners sugar. Yield about two dozen.

Dreams and Nightmares

Her eyes opened slowly, almost reluctantly. She really didn't want to wake up, she just wanted to drift in that in-between time when you're not asleep and you're not awake, to revel in the joy of last night. This by far she thought was the best time of her life. Was it all just a dream? The room was dark except for a slender beam of sunlight that peeped through a small opening of the drawn curtain. She looked at her hand and the beautiful diamond ring and sighed with delight. She then turned and looked toward the dresser and there it was, off to the corner, sort of basking in the little bit of sunshine that shone right on it, the trophy her peers had given her. No, she happily sighed, last night was real.

She stretched and reached for Beau's pillow. The scent of his aftershave lotion still lingered on the pillowcase, as she hugged it close to her heart. "Beau, is so sweet," she whispered, "I do love him; it's always been him. Now my heart understands what my soul has always known."

She looked at the ring again and marveled at how spectacular it was. Small baguettes surrounded the very large blue diamond. It was all the more special to her because of its history. Four generations ago Beau's great, great, great grandfather, the Duke D'Rampart had given this very same ring to his young bride. Now it's hers and it made her feel closer to her soon to be new family.

Last night was wonderful she thought again, but today is here and I must get up and get dressed. She sat up in bed and stretched trying to shake off this reverie she felt.

I have so much to do, she thought and just a few days to get it all done. She bounced out of bed, her long slim legs taking large strides toward the shower as she mentally made notes of the errands she must run.

Let's see, I'll go to Royal Street first and pick up the antique china I spotted in the window the other night when the shop was closed. Then just two streets down was a gallery that looked interesting, that I really should check out.

After her shower she hurriedly dressed in lilac slacks and a short sleeved white embroidered blouse. She tied her hair loosely back with a lilac ribbon, which made her look more like a teenager then a successful restaurateur.

She smiled as she picked up Shabante's gris-gris, placed it around her neck and said to the mirror, "I'll wear this gris-gris for luck." She slipped her watch on her wrist and noted that the time was ten minutes after nine. Hmm, she thought I should be back in time for lunch with Beau. He said his meeting with Dunbar Jones would take long, but it was too important to miss.

She picked up her small purse that had only enough room for her checkbook and identification. She was just about to leave, when she remembered her promise to Etienne about the cell phone. She reached for the phone and clipped it to her waistband. "There," she said out loud, "Now I've kept my promise."

She checked her watch again, and with a light heart and a smile on her face she thought, I should be back in plenty of time. With that she left the room. Unaware that her life as she knew it was about to drastically change.

Janelle walked out of the hotel and asked the doorman for directions to the antique shop. He told her to walk down Royal Street, turn left and walk three blocks to Iverville. Sure enough there was the little shop she had noticed the other night.

What a beautiful day, she thought. The sun is out, the humidity is low, and life is so good.

She entered the antique shop and went straight to the china she had spotted in the window. What luck, she thought, it's still available. As she was inspecting the dishes, a distinguished looking man approached her and said, "It's beautiful isn't it?

"Oh yes, it really is."

"I could see that you have excellent taste. Not only is this pattern beautiful, but I must tell you that there is a legend that is associated wit this particular china."

Janelle smiled and said, "Now I'm always fascinated by a good story, please tell me all about it."

"Well rumor has it that Lafitte and his bank of pirates, were all invited to Andrew Jackson's house for dinner. You see Jackson really needed their help in defeating the British in the war of 1812. He knew that the British were planning a full-scale attack, and if they were successful they would gain control of the Mississippi waterways. Of course Jackson could not allow this to happen. Now the British soldiers were all expertly trained, they had just fought Napoleon and were very experienced. However, Jackson's army consisted of a handful of soldiers, mostly volunteers from the area. The rest were inexperienced free men of color, woman and children. It was a sad excuse for an army."

"It sounds like it. When you stop to think about it, what chance could they possibly have had against a trained army," Janelle said as she sat down at a Baroque antique desk.

"Well he was aware that the pirates knew the water-ways, like the back of their hands, and Andrew Jackson was certain that without their help he would surely lose the battle. He decided to invite them to dinner so he could persuade them to help him. He served that dinner on this very china."

"Did it work?"

"Fortunately for us yes. It seemed that Lafitte was weary of operating outside of the law, and knew it was only a matter of time before he and his fellow pirates were caught and hung. He told Mr. Jackson that he wanted to live in a nice house have fine furniture, to hold soirees served with beautiful china. In other words he longed to be respectable."

"What did Jackson do?"

"Why, he did the only thing he could do; remember he desperately needed their help. He offered the pirates full pardons in exchange for their loyalty. The Pirates agreed, and did their part, by standing watch over the inlands, and warning them of the British arrival by sea. They helped the army dig mud ramparts so when the British attacked the bullets entered the mud, not the American soldiers. The battle lasted less then two hours. When morning came the Americans were amazed at the sea of dead and wounded British soldiers. The British casualties exceeded two thousand. The American reported thirteen casualties. What was left of the British troops retreated to Lake Borgn. So, Andrew Jackson, and Jean Lafitte both got what they wanted, and they came to their mutual agreement over dinner, while eating off of this very same china."

"That's a wonderful story," said Janelle. "This tale would surly entertain my customers. Would you happen to know what kind of food was served that day?"

"You know, I believe I do have that information for you, I know it's here somewhere," as he rummaged through his desk drawer looking thru history magazines. "As you can tell I'm quite a history buff."

"I wanted to buy the china because of the various flowers in the pattern. That's what attracted me to it, especially the crimson one. It reminded me of a flower that grows wild back home. Now that I know of the marvelous legend behind it, I must have it. It's a bargain at this price. I would like it sent to my place of business in Crestview California, is that O.K?"

"Not a problem at all. I'll make sure it's packed really well, and I'll give you a copy of the dinner menu they had that historical night."

As she handed him her charge card she looked up and saw a woman looking at her through the window. Something stirred inside her and she thought she possible knew her, but it was impossible to tell because she was wearing a large hat, and had on dark sunglasses.

She handed the clerk her identification, turned back to the window and the woman was gone. Was it just her imagination? All this talk about danger from Shabante really had her spooked.

The clerk smiled, gave her back her card, and said, "The shipment should take about five days, and I must say it's been a pleasure doing business with you."

"I just love southern hospitality," smiled Janelle. "By the way do you know of any interesting galleries close by?"

"Well, the gallery around the corner is very good, but if you want a bargain, and if you don't mind a short walk there is a marvelous one, not much further sort of off the beaten path, that has some wonderful finds. Because of the location it is very inexpensive."

"Now that I like," she laughed, "I'm always interested in a bargain."

"Just take Iverville Street to Clinton and it's on the right side of the street. It's called Madame Du Buas."

"Thanks so much, I'll check it out."

"By the way," he said very charmingly, "Southern hospitality comes easy when dealing with tourists as charming as you."

She blushed and waved as she left the shop. She stopped outside the door and checked her watch, ten thirty, now that didn't take long at all. I think I'll just about have enough time to check out Madam Du Buas, and still be able to meet Beau on schedule.

She walked quickly down the street following his instructions. As she walked fear started creeping over her as she noticed how drastically the neighborhood had changed. It's so deserted here, she thought; there is no one in sight. She heard footsteps behind her, but when she turned around there wasn't anyone there.

She started walking faster as the fear inside her intensified to the point where she felt like the hair on the back of her head was standing up. Janelle started to run faster and faster, she found it hard to breathe, her chest felt as though it was going to burst. She couldn't seem to fill her lungs with enough air. She almost fell as her ankle turned on the uneven brick street. She steadied herself, started running again and heard a whizzing sound go past her ear.

"Oh God help me its true isn't it? Someone does want to hurt me." She was terrified and running as fast as she could, while holding onto the gris-gris around her neck. She remembered Shabante's words, "you must look behind you!"

She turned her head and saw a man holding a gun that was aimed at her. She tripped on a stone, and almost fell as her body lunged forward. She heard two popping sounds only this time she felt like her head was exploding. Her arm jerked so hard she pulled the gris-gris off of the long cord. Her hand touched her burning temple and she saw it was full of blood. She looked down at the bright red stain on her blouse, and fell to the sidewalk as her eyes rolled up back in her head. Her purse and the gris-gris in her hand dropped to the sidewalk as she mercifully collapsed and became unconscious.

When she awoke for a moment she heard footsteps, and smelled cigarette smoke, just like in her nightmare. She saw a very dirty looking young man pick up her purse and jam it into his jacket pocket. She was frozen with fear as she closed her eyes hoping he would go away.

He bent over her, his lips parted in a sinister smile, as he saw a small pool of blood starting to form on the concrete. "Good," he said, "she is as good as dead."

Janelle regained consciousness, looked at him and screamed, when she saw his eyes, the same eyes that had always awakened her in her nightmares. They were the eyes of a frog. So cold and empty looking, they left her shaking with fear.

He threw his cigarette onto the sidewalk, aimed the gun at her heart and was about to pull the trigger when he heard voices coming from the nearby courtyard. He looked up and down the street, and saw a curtain move in a nearby window. It's too dangerous, he thought, I don't want to get caught; besides she's a goner anyway. He quickly walked away.

She lay there on the sidewalk, quiet still, while the pool of blood slowly widened. "Wake up." said the voice in her ear. "Don't you hear my chimes calling you?"

She moaned softly, content to be unconscious, not wanting to face the pain of reality. "You must wake up, you have work to do," said the voice.

The chimes from the church nearby awakened her, almost as if they were calling her home. She slowly stood up and although dazed started to slowly walk the two blocks down Chartres to the St. Louis Cathedral, toward the bells.

She stumbles a few times, supporting herself on the side of the buildings, as the bells kept calling to her. "I'm coming," she whispered. She knew deep down that she must find the church. Her long red hair had come loose and now covering her face and her partially blood stained blouse. She heard the chimes again and knew she was close to safety. Oh God please guide me, she prayed, as she turned the corner and found the old church.

Tears of relief were slowly sliding down her cheeks, when she heard the singing coming from the old church. "I found it," she whispered, "I'll be safe there, I'm so tired now." As she entered the church, she heard the song the choir was singing and the words filled her with strength, for she knew they were meant for her.

"I have heard my people cry, all who dwell in dark and sin, my hand will save. I who made the stars of night, I will make their darkness bright. Who will I send? Here I am Lord. It is I Lord. I have heard you calling in the night. I will go Lord if you lead me. I will hold your people in my heart."

Janelle groped her way to the nearest pew, and thankfully fell to her knees. The church was filled with nuns and priests all on their knees fervently praying for the salvation of the church against the invading termites. The sound of the soprano singing filled Janelle with an overwhelming sense of peace, as the beautiful voice echoed throughout the church.

"It's lovely here," murmured Janelle, "I'll rest a minute, suddenly I feel so tired." She rested her head on the back of the pew in front of her. Blood from her wound slowly dripped onto the seat.

"Lord, have mercy," said the priest. Between hymns, and the priest's prayers, you could hear ever so faintly the drops of blood falling from Janelle's wounds as they hit the wooden seat in front of her.

"Lord, have mercy," responded the nuns.

"I feel safe here, thank you lord for helping me find this wonderful old church," she whispered weakly.

"Grant us you salvation," said the priest.

Drip, drip as the pool of blood widened.

"Amen," said the nun.

The young nun next to Janelle whispered, "In the name of the father, the son and the holy spirit, amen," as she made the sign of the cross. She opened her eyes unto the pool of blood that had collected on the bench in front of her. A cry of fear escapes from her throat, as she covered her mouth with her hand.

The Mother Superior angrily turned around to scold the young nun, and saw this pretty girl next to her covered with blood and almost unconscious.

"Mother of God," she whispered, "she is hurt. Quickly sisters take this poor child into the rectory. Sister Gertrude run and find Sister Agnes, we need her nursing skills. Hurry now, she shook the young nun by the shoulders, snap out of it, run!"

Sister Gertrude pulled herself together, and ran searching for Sister Agnes. The other nuns wedged their bodies under Janelle's arms, and carried her into the rectory.

As they placed her on the sofa, Janelle moaned in pain.

"Hurry Sister Agnes," said the young nun as she took the nurse's hand and literally pulled her along the back of the old church. "The Poor girl needs you, Oh Sweet Mother of God, I hope she is still alive."

"I'm walking as fast as I can," said Sister Agnes sounding out of breathe, "You know I'm not as young as you."

"It's awful, there is blood everywhere, oh please hurry." As they ran along the back of the church, they didn't notice the attractive young woman standing in the shadow of the statue of St. Dymphna, the patron saint of the mentally ill.

Mala's eyes narrowed as she watched the two nuns enter the rectory, an expression of quiet rage flowed over her. Her fists clenched and her lips turned from a smile into a sinister sneer. I know where you're at, she thought, and I'll be back for you. She turned with great determination and walked out of the church.

The rectory suddenly became very busy with nuns running to fill the orders given by Mother Superior. She sent one nun for towels, one for hot soapy water, and one for a blanket.

"Thank God you're here Sister Agnes, she looks so pale," said Mother Superior looking very concerned. "She is such a pretty young thing to have to face so much pain."

"Let's see how bad the wound is," said Sister Agnes, as she started to cut Janelle's blouse open to get a good look at the wound. She washed away the blood with hot soapy water, than sterilized the wound with peroxide. She stopped the bleeding on her forehead, but her arm required stitches.

"It doesn't look bad at all," she said. "The bullet grazed the forehead, she was lucky, it could have been worse. The bullet entered and exited through the fleshy part of her arm.

See Mother Superior, right through here," as she showed her the wound.

"I know I've cleaned it thoroughly, and I'm not worried about infection. All she needs now is lots of rest. I've given her a sedative that should keep her sleeping for hours. Does anyone know who she is?"

"No," says Mother Superior. It looks like the poor child came to the church for shelter."

"You are aware Mother Superior, that the injury was a gun shot wound. The law requires that we call the police," said Sister Agnes.

"Yes, I know, the law sister, but the child came to the church for help. When she wakes we will call the police, until then we'll protect her. Sister Gertrude and Sister Catherine, the two of you stay with her until she wakes up and tells us who she is. Now let's make her comfortable and let her rest."

"Yes of course," said the two nuns in unison, "we will pray for her," as they pulled out their rosary.

"I'll send in your dinners and lots of coffee to keep you awake, but under no circumstances are you to leave her alone," said Mother Superior, as she left the room.

The Pirates Dinner
Roast Squab with Oyster-Giblet Dressing

Giblets from Squabs or Rock Cornish Game Hens
½ cup chopped celery
¼ cup of butter
2 tbs. snipped parsley
1/8 tsp pepper
1/8 tsp. of crushed dried thyme
Cooking Oil
1/3 cup of finely chopped onion
½ pint of shucked oysters
½ tsp. salt
1/8 tsp. of crushed dried rosemary
3 cups of dried bread cubes
Six- 12 to 14ozs Squabs or Rock Cornish game hens.
1/3 cups dry white wine

Chop the giblets from the Squabs or Cornish hens. In a large saucepan cook chopped celery, onion and giblets in butter till tender about 10 minutes. Stir in the undrained oysters and snipped parsley. Cook 5 minutes more. Stir in salt, pepper, rosemary, and thyme. Add dry bread cubes and mix thoroughly. Sprinkle the inside of squabs or hens with salt. Stuff each of the birds with some of the dressing. Brush skin with cooking oil. Place the stuffed birds, breast side up, on rack in shallow roasting pan. Roast uncovered at 400 degrees until done. 40 to 50 minutes. Baste the birds frequently with dry white wine. Makes 6 servings.

Old Southern Beaten Biscuits

2 cups of all-purpose flour
1 tsp. sugar
½ tsp. salt
¼ tsp. baking powder
1/8 tsp. of cream of tartar
¼ cup lard
¾ to 1-cup ice water
Butter

In a small bowl stir together flour, sugar, salt, baking powder and cream of tartar. Cut in the lard till mixture resembles coarse crumbs. Make a well in center of dry mixture. Add ¾ cup of ice water to make dough stiff.

Turn the dough out onto a lightly floured surface. Beat vigorously with the flat side of a wooden or metal mallet for 15 minutes, turning and folding the dough constantly. Roll or pat the dough to ¼ inch thickness. Cut the dough with floured 2-inch biscuit cutter; dip the cutter in four between cuts to prevent sticking.

Place the biscuits on ungreased baking sheet. Prick the tops of each biscuit 3 times with a fork. Bake at 400 degrees until crisp and lightly browned about 20 minutes. Serve biscuits warm with butter makes about 24.

Clam Fritters with Wine Sauce

1 dozen minced clams

1 cup all purpose flour

2 tsp. baking powder

Fat for frying

½ tsp. salt

1 beaten egg

Milk

Creamy Wine Sauce

Drain clams, reserving liquid. Add milk to liquid to equal 2/3 cup. Stir together flour, baking powder and the salt. Combine the milk mixture, drained clams and beaten egg. Stir into the dry ingredients just till moistened.

Carefully drop by tablespoonfuls in to deep hot fat 365 degrees. Fry six to eight fritters at a time until golden, 2 to 3 minutes. Drain on paper toweling. Serve immediately with Creamy Wine Sauce. Makes 6 servings.

Creamy Wine Sauce

In a small saucepan melt 2 tablespoons butter. Blend in 3 tablespoons all-purpose flour and ¼ teaspoon seasoned salt. Add 1 cup of light cream or milk all at once. Cook, stirring constantly, till mixture is thickened and bubbly. Stir some of the hot mixture into 1 slightly beaten egg yolk; return to remaining hot mixture. Stir in 3 tablespoons dry white wine and 2 tablespoons chopped pimiento. Heat through.

Lemon Cake

1-1/2 cups granulated sugar
½ cup butter
1-1/2 tsp. grated lemon peel
3 eggs
2-1/2 cups all purpose flour
½ tsp. baking soda
½ cup milk
¼ cup lemon juice
2 cups sifted powdered sugar
½ tsp. vanilla
milk

In a mixing bowl cream together granulated sugar, butter and 1 tsp. lemon peel till fluffy. Add eggs, one at a time, beating well after each addition. Stir together flour and soda; add to the creamed mixture alternately with the milk, beating after each addition. Beat in the lemon juice. Turn the mixture into a greased and lightly floured 13x9x2 inch-baking dish. Bake at 350 degrees till cake tests done, about 25 minutes. Cool thoroughly.

Stir together sifted powdered sugar, remaining lemon peel and vanilla; stir in enough milk about 2 tablespoons to make glaze of spreading consistency. Spread the glaze on cooled cake.

The Search

Beau made his way back up to the room after his meeting with Dunbar. Now that went fast, it's not quite eleven, he thought. He felt better knowing that Dunbar was aware of the situation, and on the job. He inserted the electronic key card in the door, turned the handle and said, "Janelle I'm back, and I'm going to take you to the most wonderful lunch you've ever had."

The silence in the room was deafening. He checked the bedroom, and the bathroom all the while calling her name. For the first time in his life, he knew the feeling of fear. He immediately dialed Dunbar's number. It seemed to take forever before he answered, even though it couldn't be more then ten seconds.

"Hi, this is Dunbar."

"Dunbar she's gone. We've got to find her."

"Relax Beau, she probably went shopping or to the beauty shop, you know how women are."

"I know you think I'm over reacting, and I must sound like a fool, but I'm scared. I simply can't have anything happen to her Dunbar, not now."

"OK, you check the hotel I'll start investigating the stores that are in the area, to see if anyone has seen her."

"I'll call you as soon as I hear anything, thanks Dunbar."

Beau checked the beauty shop, showed her picture to the housekeeping staff, asked the girl in the gift shop if she had seen her, so far nothing. He then showed her picture to the staff at the front desk, one young man remembered her talking to the doorman.

He felt relieved that finally some one had seen her. A chill went through him as he thought of how really invisible we all are in life. He then stepped outside and approached the doorman with Janelle's picture. "Excuse me, but it's very important that I find this girl, I believe her life might be in danger, could you take a look at this photo for me?

The doorman took the photo, and said, "Sure I saw her, it's impossible to forget someone so pretty and nice. You said her life might be threatened, now who would want to hurt such a nice person?"

"When did you see her?"

"Why, let's see. I think it was around nine fifteen or nine thirty. She wanted directions to an antique shop on Iberville. She sure looked pretty in her white blouse."

"Great! You remembered what she wore. Did she wear a skirt or slacks?"

"Light purple slacks like the color of lilacs, I remember because she had tied her hair back with the same color ribbon. She is such a nice lady to be in so much trouble. I hope you find her."

Beau immediately dialed Dunbar's number, and told him that Janelle was last seen walking to an antique shop on Ivberville and Royal. He described what she was wearing, and said he would meet him at the shop. Beau ran as fast as he could, arriving there at the same time as Dunbar, who was breathing quite heavily.

"I've just got to start cutting down on my calories, man I'm out of shape."

"You're still the best Dunbar, let's go in and find out what we can. I think we're getting close to finding her."

Of course the clerk remembered her, and was very distraught to think that such a lovely person would be in danger. That's my Janelle; everyone she speaks to loves her, thought Beau. She is unforgettable. Please God let me find her unharmed, he silently prayed.

"You know," said the clerk as he frowned trying to remember every detail. "I remember she had asked me about galleries in the area, and I told her about Madame Du Bua's over on Clinton Street. You might want to check there."

Beau looked at his watch, two o'clock. He tried calling Etienne, but his cell phone was out of the calling area. "Come on," Dunbar said, "let's check out the gallery."

After a few blocks they noticed how seedy this section of town was. "I know something has happened to her Dunbar, I feel it."

"Yeah, I know, I have the same vibes, and it's not good." Dunbar's eyes squinted as if to focus. His head slowly turned as he scanned every small detail of his surroundings. He saw the street, curbs, sidewalks, and walls, looking for clues, not wanting to miss anything that was unusual.

Beau started to walk south when Dunbar took hold of his arm, and said, "Beau look over there, across the street by the corner, it's a lilac ribbon, right there on the sidewalk. Do you see it?"

"Yes, it is! Oh God, Dunbar, I'm scared." When they ran to the corner, Beau went straight to the ribbon. As he started to pick it up, he noticed all the blood. "Oh no, Dunbar," he cried out, "look there's blood near the ribbon, and over there is Janelle's gris-gris, that Shabante gave her."

"Don't touch the ribbon, or anything, else, come step away, right now Beau." Said Dunbar as he pulled out his cell phone and dialed his captain. He filled him in on the details, and requested a C.S.I. unit. Within minutes the street was filled with crime scene analysts, and detectives.

Dunbar had directed the officers to secure the area by marking it with yellow tape and posting officers outside the tape. It is a known fact that some of the biggest contaminants of crime scenes are police officers, ambulance attendants and firemen. It is important to locate the original crime scene. Dunbar knew this and made sure Beau did not disturb anything.

The Crime Scene Analyst carefully walked into the taped area and took several photographs of everything, to record the conditions and evidence of the scene.

"Beau buddy," said Dunbar, as he placed his hand on Beau's shoulder. "Just hang in there we should know something soon."

Beau looked at Dunbar, and said, "It's hopeless isn't it? I mean there were no witnesses." He shook his head back and forth, raised his shoulders as if to question, and said, "What could they possible find out from just a ribbon and a pool of blood?"

"That's where you're wrong Beau, there was a witness, but it's a silent one. Let me explain," Dunbar said as he frowned. "When I first entered Law Enforcement, I thought that my heightened sense of smell and sight was all I needed. I have learned differently. You see wherever the perpetrator had stepped, or touched, he leaves, unconsciously a silent witness against him.

There are fingerprints, footprints, hair, fibers from clothing, and the pattern of blood splashes, all bear witness against him. It is factual evidence. They could tell how tall the attacker is, how much he weighs, the color of his hair, his race, and much more. All of this is from the clues that they are now finding."

"How can they tell how tall someone is?"

"Do you see how close the ribbon was to the wall? Do you see how there are tiny blood splatters on the wall?"

"Yes," said Beau looking very pale, winching as he looked at the wall.

"Well that tells us how tall the perpetrator is. Hang in there my friend I'm going to check on what they know." Dunbar leaned over the tape and asked the specialist what he had found so far.

"Well, he said while taking notes of the pattern of the blood splatters, "Someone was definitely attacked on this spot." He pointed to the pool of blood on the sidewalk and also the splatter of blood along the wall. "We are measuring the splatter to determine the height of the perpetrator. Until we find a body, I really don't know how serious the attack was. We did bag three thirty eight caliber shell casings which might have a print or two on them. We'll run the casings through the computer and compare them to other crimes that may have been committed with the gun that was used. There was a cigarette butt found that we bagged for a D.N.A., which we could find out from the saliva. We also picked up a partial shoe print. It looks like he may have stepped in some of the blood when he left the scene.

"Please let me know as soon as you can what you find out, it's kind of personal," Dunbar said as he shook hands with the expert. "You've got my cell phone number, call me anytime."

Beau watched the professionals doing their job and was amazed at how thorough they were. Not only did the analyst expert photograph everything, he also took samples of the blood. With tongs he picked up the evidence and bagged the ribbon and the gris-gris, he vacuumed up any fibers or hair that he could find on the sidewalk near the blood. Whatever was bagged of course was marked with crime scene location, the date and his initials.

The sidewalk was then dusted for prints, and photographed. There was a smudged bloody palm print; they dusted it, and photographed it. They couldn't be sure about the smudged print until they looked at the photograph under a microscope.

"Beau," said Dunbar, "I checked out the gallery, Janelle never made it that far. Whatever has happened to her happened right on this spot. I really think it's very hopeful that we might still find her alive. I'm having the detectives knock on all doors in the area, we're showing copies of her picture and of course we are checking all the nearby hospitals. You never know, maybe someone found her, and took her for help."

Darkness was starting to fall, and still no sign of Janelle. Dunbar made Beau go back to the hotel, to check again with the doorman to see if he could remember anything else. Dunbar knew the doorman didn't know anything, but it was a way of keeping him busy.

The detectives couldn't find anyone who had seen her. Now as twilight set in, the street was once again coming alive. Dunbar walked back to Bourbon Street feeling so helpless. Beau was one of his best friends, and he would give anything to help him find this very special young woman. She has been missing since morning, and he knew time was of the essence. It is a fact that with each hour that passes, the trail becomes colder.

Crowds of people were now pouring into the French Quarter. Good thing it wasn't a holiday, or special event, that would really be a mess. During Jazz Fest or Mardi-Gra, the crowds are so thick you couldn't move. During those times hotel rooms in the city of New Orleans were at a premium.

To accommodate the overflow, the police department tows every car in the pound, over to the side streets. They place blankets and pillows in the cars to accommodate those without a room. Who says a big city doesn't have a heart?

Dunbar leaned against the wall outside a nightclub on Bourbon Street and started searching the crowds with his eyes hoping against hope he would find something, some small clue. He noticed only the usual, a few boisterous college students from Toulaine planning to crash a party at a nearby apartment, two lovers hugging each other under the street-lamp, he could read the young man's lips as he asked the girl to marry him. The tearful girl nodded yes.

His eyes moved on to a middle aged couple, they were tourists visiting New Orleans for the very first time. He could see the woman talking to her husband, smiling and saying. "Isn't this exciting Mel? Look at all these people, dancing in the street. Oh, I love this music; listen to that trumpet player. Don't you love it?"

"I hate the crowd, drunken people all over the place!" He was telling her in no uncertain terms. "The stupid music is too darn loud and once we get back to Idaho you'll never get me out of my Lazy Boy chair. Watching television in my own living room, that's a good time. Damn," he said," my feet are killing me. This is the only place I've ever seen where you have to walk everywhere."

Oh well, thought Dunbar, as he laughed, different strokes for different folks. I guess some people want to spend the rest of their life traveling, learning something new, while others want to live it in a vacuum; afraid of new places and different things, or maybe they are afraid of life and would rather wither away in familiar surroundings.

Now looky here thought Dunbar. Two guys arguing over that good-looking blonde. What's this? His eyes narrowed in on a very dirty looking young man talking to a young lady with dark glasses. He knew he was onto something because the hair on his arms and the back of his neck was sticking up; it always did when his intuition was on target.

He started reading the lips of the girl, and immediately knew she was talking about Janelle. "You didn't finish the job," she said to the dirty man, as a few people walked in front of Dunbar's view. He inched closer so he could continue reading their lips.

"I did do it," the man said, "She was as good as dead. I saw her—"

"You didn't see anything you idiot! What did you use to do it?" Dunbar's heart started pounding as he stood riveted, afraid to move, afraid they might spot him.

"I bought a gun, an R.G. 38 caliber it was expensive, what they call a Saturday night special. I'm telling you she was dying right there on the sidewalk. There was blood everywhere. I swear it! Now give me my money."

Every nerve in Dunbar's body wanted to scream, I found them! He hit the stored number for Beau on his cell phone, without ever taking his eyes off of the unlikely pair.

"Beau I found them. I just read their lips. I'm across the street from Dirty Sally's bar. The guy is telling an attractive woman who must be Mala that he shot Janelle. He is now demanding the rest of his money. She told him she wants to see the gun. He just pulled it out of his jacket and handed it to her, right in front of hundreds of people, and no one is paying any attention to them but me."

"You said this gun is expensive? You're a liar!" screamed Mala.

"Beau, Mala just took the gun and she is pointing it at him. She's saying. "You jerk you didn't kill her. I saw her walk into the church. I guess when you want a job done right you've got to do it yourself, and now that I have the gun that's exactly what I'm going to do."

"Listen lady that's all right with me, just give me my money, and you'll never see me again."

"I'm not paying you anything, you creep. But you're right about one thing I'm never going to see you again." She then stuck the gun in his chest and pulled the trigger. A look of surprise and then disbelief came over the young man as he collapsed onto the sidewalk.

"Beau, she just shot him, he is falling to the ground, and I've got to get over to him."

"I'm almost there. I'm only a block away. Dunbar, if she was able to walk into the church, she must be all right." exclaimed a very relieved Beau.

Dunbar ran to stop Mala but she had successfully managed to disappear into the crowd. Due to his extraordinarily sharpened senses, he could still smell the scent of her perfume, "It's Jasmine, I'm sure of it," he said to himself. He waved to a police officer friend of his for help, as he then called in a code 415A (assault/battery with a gun). They requested an ambulance, but after closer examination changed it to a coroner's wagon. The Toad was dead.

Beau arrived on the scene as Dunbar was going through the dead man's pockets. He pulled out Janelle's purse with her identification in it. "Look Beau, it's Janelle's purse. I know she's alive. Mala said she saw her walk into the church."

"Which church?" Beau was shaking with anticipation of taking Janelle in his arms and never letting go. He was so afraid she might be seriously hurt and he wanted to be there with her.

"I don't know. Let me think, oh yeah, I believe there are only three in this area. We'll just check them all. We have to do this fast, Mala knows which church, we don't. Come on I've got a squad car around the corner. We can start with the closest one."

As they climbed into the car Beau's cell phone rang. "Hello," he said rather apprehensively.

"Beau, it's me Etienne. I'm driving back to town from Baton Rouge when I heard the messages you left me. What's going on? Did you find Janelle?"

"No not yet. We know she was attacked, because we found some of her belongings in a pool of blood."

"Did you find the cell phone? She promised she would never leave the hotel room without it."

"Etienne I forgot all about that, I'll call that number right away. We know she was last seen walking into a church. We're on our way to check them out now."

"I'll catch up with you, the minute I'm in town. Good luck Beau, I hope you fine her."

"Thanks Etienne, I know we will, we just have to find her."

Beau dialed the number, the phone rang once, twice, three, four times and just as he was about to hang up, a very timid voice whispered, "Hello? This is Sister Agnes."

"Sister, my name is Beau Rampart. I'm desperately looking for a red haired young lady, who's...

"Yes, yes, she is here right now, at the St. Louis Cathedral, but she is still asleep," replied the nun excitedly.

"Thank you God," said Beau as he swallowed a couple of times to hold back the sob that was caught in his throat all day. He turned to Dunbar and said, "She's at the St. Louis Cathedral."

"Beau, caution them to be careful, we'll be there in about seven minutes."

"Sister, tell me, is she all right?" said Beau in a very shaky voice.

"She was shot, poor thing, in the shoulder, it's not serious. The wound was cleaned and bandaged. She was given a sedative to make her sleep. She should be waking up very soon."

"Sister Agnes, please listen carefully. Her life is in danger. I need you to look out for her. There is a very dangerous young woman who wants to kill her. She was last seen wearing a large hat and dark glasses. Be very cautious, she has a gun, and she is not afraid to use it. We're only a few minutes away. Please be very careful." He placed the cell phone back into his pocket silently praying for Janelle's safety, while the squad car raced to the church.

The Shooting

Mala's mind raced as she walked the few blocks to the church with the gun safely tucked away in her purse. She was anxious to use it.

Pay him? Pay him for what? He got what he deserved, that no good stupid low life. I did him a favor; he's definitely better off dead. He was just too dirty to live. The world is better off without that incompetent cheating idiot.

She walked with great determination toward the church. Her mind so full of hate she didn't even notice the cars swerving to miss her as she crossed the street. Mala was always her main focus; she was the only one that mattered in the universe, and everyone better just get out of her way.

I'll kill her myself. I know where they put her, it was in the room to the side of the alter. If the stupid nuns think they can hide her, they are mistaken. I'll get rid of her all by myself, and then we will just see about Beau.

The tour buses had been pulling in and out of St. Louis Cathedral for most of the day and well into the night. Each bus was crowded with priests and nuns, who took turns praying for the old church. Father O'Rielly and his parishioners had been planning the prayer vigil for the last six months. The schools were turned into dormitories with sleeping mats for the over 200 nuns and 70 priests who had been arriving from all sections of the country.

It was a time for the clergy to socialize, to visit old friends, make new ones, and save the old church through the power of prayer.

The church was packed; with standing room only. The sound of the rosary beads clicking through the fingers of the nuns was almost like background music accompanying the chanting of the priest.

Mala stood in the doorway, eyeing the rectory half hidden behind the altar. That's where she's at, she thought, as the rage within her accelerated. She saw the priest at the pulpit preaching to the congregation, as all eyes were facing him. Oh great, I'll never be able to reach the rectory with this crowd, I've got to think, I need a plan as she turned and walked out into the hall. She walked over to the water fountain and took a drink hoping it would make her think a little clearer. She looked up and noticed a young nun walk into the washroom alone. That's it. All I need is a disguise so I could reach the rectory without being stopped, and what better disguise then to become a nun, she smiled at her cleverness as she quickly followed the nun into the washroom and locked the door behind her. The young nun turned to look at her as her smile froze on her face when she saw the gun.

"Look sister, I have nothing against you, but I just have to have your little nuns outfit, and I need it now!"

The smile on the nuns face vanished as she stared at the gun. She had seen it often enough in Bosnia to last her a lifetime; but she never in a million years expected to face danger again; especially in this wonderful holy church. The memory flashed in her mind as she remembered that horrible time a few years ago, as she watched her mother and brother gunned down by the soldiers, while she hid under the stairs trying not scream, hands pressed tightly over her mouth. A priest, who knew her family, had come by to check on them, and found her the next day, still hiding under the stairs, whimpering in silence. She was sent to live with the nuns, but it took her a long time before she talked again. Gradually she began to live again, without fear, protected within the walls of the monastery. She understood the violence during the time of war; but here in this old church?

"Did you hear what I said? I want your little nun's outfit and I want it now".

The nun heard Mala's angry words, saw the gun being waved in her face, and for a moment in time relived her childhood memories of war. But this time it was different; she was different, she had an inner strength that took over her mind and body as her hands dropped to her side and she felt the cool touch of the rosary beads hanging from her waist, reassuring her to stay calm.

Now! I said I want you nuns outfit now!

"Of course, it's O.K. I could tell you're serious, the young nun said with a smile. I'll help you, tell me what's wrong, and I'll find Father O'Rielly, he'll help you with your problem. Now put the gun away please; you don't need to hurt anyone, I promise I'll help you."

"Save the sermon, sister. You do as I say and I won't hurt you. Take off your habit. That's right, now your top, good, and now your skirt. This will do just fine".

The young nun stood shivering as she stood in her slip silently praying for guidance.

"Step into the stall," said Mala in a menacing whisper. As the nun turned and did what she was told, Mala took the handle of the gun, slammed it onto the back of the nuns head, knocking her unconscious. She quickly put the habit on and the skirt over her clothes. She put the gun into her pocket, and discarded her purse in the trashcan covered with paper towels. She looked at her reflection in the mirror, and was surprised that she looked like a nun. Maybe a little too much makeup but all in all if she walked fast with her head down, she just might pull it off.

Mala noticed the out of order sign in the corner, the one they use when they are cleaning the floors; perfect she thought as she pushed it into the hallway and positioned it in front of the door. "Now" she whispered to the empty hall, "it's time to take care of that nobody red head." She entered the church and walked very quickly up the aisle, pushing aside anyone in her way; determined to finish the job the Toad started and muffed.

Dunbar and Beau reached the old church and surveyed the crowd. "Beau you take the right and I'll take the left."

"Right" Beau reached out and touched his friends arm and said very seriously, "you have no idea how grateful I am that you're with me. I just couldn't face this alone."

"No problem buddy, just find Mala before she causes anymore harm." Dunbar went to the left side of the church, took a deep breath and prayed that his sensitive senses would help him solve this problem. He started to scan the crowded church looking for any sign of something that was not in sync, that unsettling one thing that didn't fit in.

People were trying to find seats in the crowded church, nuns, priests and parishioners were standing in the back, and off to the side. How could we find her in this crowd, he thought, as he shook his head, it's close to impossible. Suddenly he was pushed aside by a nun, he apologized for being in the way, but she just hurriedly walked past him. She was halfway up the aisle when Dunbar's sense of smell kicked in with the scent of Jasmine. "That's her, it's the nun!" He starred at her shoes and saw the heels, and quickly started to run after her.

Beau noticed that Dunbar was almost running down the aisle. He must be after the nun that just went into the rectory that was to the side of the altar. Beau crossed over to the other aisle, and followed right behind Dunbar.

The two nuns gasped and stood up abruptly as Mala came bursting into the room waving the gun. "We were expecting you," said the older nun.

"Good, I'd hate to disappoint anyone. Well, I'm here. Now where is she?"

"You should leave now," said the nun very quietly, "the police will be here any minute."

"Yeah, right" Mala looked at her as though she was crazy. "The police don't know anything about me. Now get out of my way."

"Please, for your own sake, leave now before anyone gets hurt. We just received a phone call. Honestly, the police will be here any minute. Leave now and you won't get into any more trouble."

Mala became confused. She hadn't eaten anything in two days, and had trouble focusing. Not once, had she ever contemplated repercussions for her actions. She had assumed that because of her father's power, she wouldn't have to answer to anyone ever.

"Trouble, what trouble could I possibly have? Don't you know who I am? My father can fix anything do you hear me? He could fix anything!

She heard a small cry of someone who was in pain, and saw Janelle trying to sit up from the sofa behind the nuns.

"So there she is, behind the two of you on that sofa.

Well don't worry sisters; I don't care about you. I just want to finish her off, this time for good." Moving swiftly she shoved the one nun aside.

She aimed the gun at Janelle, just as Dunbar ran into the room.

"Stop Mala!" he shouted.

It was a shock to hear her name. She turned toward Dunbar and involuntarily squeezed the trigger of the gun, just as Beau ran into the room. Beau pushed Dunbar out of the way, as the bullet entered his chest. His arms flew up, and his body collapsed on the floor, as though a sudden powerful gust of wind had knocked him over.

Mala saw the only man she had ever loved lying on the floor bleeding. She realized what she had done, dropped the gun, and ran out of the room.

Dunbar dialed 911 on his cell phone requesting an ambulance for the second time in an hour. This time tears were streaming from his eyes, as he saw his close friend wounded by a bullet that was meant for him.

"Beau buddy, hold on, help is coming." Dunbar pleaded through his tears.

Sister Agnes gently pushed Dunbar aside, as she tried to stop the bleeding from Beau's chest. She applied pressure to the wound, and silently wondered when people will learn how devastating it was to have a gun.

Janelle had staggered from the sofa, still dazed by the sedatives, saw Beau on the floor with blood flowing out of him and fainted into Dunbar's arms. He caught her as she fell into his arms like a limp rag doll. Tears brimming in his eyes he muttered, "Nice to finally meet you maam."

Saying Good Bye

Mala was devastated, as she ran out of the rectory. As soon as she was outside the church, she started to peel off the nun's habit, and discarded it in the nearby trash. The vision of beau lying there dying was more than she could endure. She aimlessly walked through the streets of the French Quarter, not knowing what to do or where to go. She only knew that she couldn't go home. She had no money with her, or credit cards. They were in the purse that she had left in the church's ladies room trashcan, covered with paper towels.

She saw a familiar liquor store and realized that she was across the street from her father's condo. She entered the store, and was thankful that the owner recognized her.

"My father, sent me to buy the most expensive wine you have," said Mala with a slight smile on her face. She knew how to be charming when she had to, and now more then ever she had to be convincing. "Oh of course he said to charge it to his account." She knew the shop's owner would be pleased by the two hundred dollar purchase, and never question, the daughter of the richest man in town.

He fawned all over her as he wrapped up the bottle. In his thick Indian accent he said, "It's my pleasure to serve you and your father, and as a special gift I am giving him a jar of imported caviar.

"Oh how sweet of you." Mala said with the brightest smile she could manage. The shopkeeper beamed with pride as Mala took her purchase left the shop and walked across the street to her father's condo. "Hi," said Mala to the door-man in a very friendly tone. "Is my father in?"

"No, not yet, he has been gone all day."

"Well, I was suppose to meet him here and of course, silly me," she said with a little giggle, "I forgot my keys. Could you be so kind as to let me in? I'm sure he should be here any minute now," as she glanced at her watch.

The doorman hesitated, he knew he shouldn't let her in, rules are rules, but then again, she was after-all the owner's daughter. "Sure," he said, "I'm sure he just got detained" He walked over to the counter, opened the drawer, and found the key.

"I knew there had to be an extra one, here you are." He was very pleased with himself as he handed her the key. "I'll inform you dad when he comes in of your arrival," he said, as he smiled.

Sure, she thought, so he could get a big tip. She smiled at the thought of what she was about to do. She entered into the spacious, expensively decorated apartment and headed straight for the bathroom.

"What a surprise I have planned for you daddy," she said to the walls. It's what he deserves, she thought, how I hate him. She stepped into the kitchen, opened the caviar and the bottle of wine. Might as well go out in style, she laughed.

She ran the bath water; stripped away her clothes placed the wine, caviar and knife on the wide ledge of the tub. Mala sat up in the steamy tub, reached for the bottle of wine, removed the cork and poured the liquid into the most expensive Waterford crystal glass she could find. After all, this was a very special occasion.

Soaking in the perfumed steamy hot bath felt wonderful, she thought, as she sipped the strong deep red cabernet. Mala took some caviar, marveling at the wonderful taste, and how well it went with the wine.

She turned picked up the small sharp paring knife that was lying next to the bottle of imported Mouton Rothchild wine which was sitting on the edge of the tub. Holding the knife she saw her reflection on the stainless steel blade, smiled and said good-bye as she cut one wrist and then the other, as she had seen her mother do so many years ago when she was just five years old.

She recalled her mother saying, "Remember Mala when you can't get what you want anymore and you want to leave this world, then do what I'm doing. It hurts far less than life does," and she could still hear her mother's insane laughter, echoing off the bathroom walls.

Mala took another sip of wine and was amazed at how similar the color was to her blood now dripping into the bath water. What a fitting end to her life watching her blood slowly leaving her body.

As she took another taste of wine, she thought of what could have been. If only things had been different. If only Beau had loved her instead of Janelle. He was the only thing in her whole life that she had ever wanted and couldn't get. She lied, cheated, did everything to get him. She went so far as to hire a total stranger, to kill Janelle. Now there was no way out. She could not live knowing that she had killed Beau, maybe if she too died, then she would be with him. She knew they would be coming soon to arrest her, but all they would find would be her perfect naked body, covered by a blanket of blood.

She raised her glass and said, "Here's to you daddy. It's all your' fault for not fixing it in the first place." She drained the glass of the warm red liquid, closed her eyes, and started to drift into unconsciousness.

As she slipped deeper into a dream like state she heard the phone ringing, then a loud banging on the bathroom door.

"Mala open the door, it's me your father. I can help you honey."

"It's too late," she whispered, "I don't want your help now." She smiled when she thought about the pain her father would feel when he found her dead.

She could hear voices from afar, and wished they would go away, and leave her alone. Didn't they know she just wanted to die?"

The banging at the door grew louder, as Tyler ordered the detectives to break it down. Tyler held onto the wall for support when he entered the bathroom, and almost fainted at the sight of his daughter sitting in a tub full of blood.

"Here she is, Oh God please help her," cried Tyler. He turned to the detectives he had brought with him and shouted, "Someone call an ambulance now!"

She heard a man's voice crying and another saying, "we have to tape up her wrists, quick, fold this wash cloth, apply pressure, good its stopping."

"Why did this happen?" moaned Tyler. "I don't understand why it has to end this way. You know I always gave her everything money could buy."

The young detective turned to him and very seriously said, "Maybe sir, you gave her too much."

The paramedics bandaged her wrists, wrapped a ter-rycloth robe around her, and carried her to the ambulance.

"I want to go with her," said Tyler as he climbed into

the vehicle. While racing to the hospital, Tyler looked at his once beautiful daughter lying on the cot so pale and thought why? She had everything fame and all that money could buy. Why would someone so attractive want to end there live over a denied love! Why?

He shook his head and said to the paramedic, who was adjusting the I.V., that was keeping Mala alive, "It seems the longer I live the more I realize that life is so very puzzling. What I thought was important, everything I have strived for money, power, and position, it was all for her." He dabbed away the tears from his eyes with his monogrammed hand-kerchief, blew his nose, and said, "They now seem so insignificant. Life really is one big mystery."

The paramedic just listened at the distraught man, and nodded his head a few times in agreement.

"You know," said Tyler, "maybe when you're born there should be a rule book to follow, so people don't get side-tracked and go down the wrong path. A book on how to live, you know? He looked quizzically at the paramedic.

The paramedic smiled, touched the crucifix hanging on a chain around his neck thought about how he saw the dark side of life every day, and wondered when if ever people were going to see the light. "Mr. Tyler," he said there is one, it was written an awfully long time ago, its' called The Bible."

Religion was the one aspect of life that was missing from Tyler's world, and it suddenly saddened him. He put his head down, rubbed his aching eyes, and for the first time in his life prayed. He prayed with all his strength for forgiveness. He prayed for guidance. "How, he asked God," how am I ever going to fix this? My only daughter has killed a man, attempted to kill Janelle, shot Beau, and tried to kill herself. She has caused so much destruction to so many lives." The only sound that could be heard was the siren blearing as the ambulance sped to the hospital. Tyler the Terrible sat starring at his daughter as his sanity now hung in the balance and with deep emotion, from the depth of his soul, he said, "Please God, help me fix this mess!"

The Waiting

Dunbar found it difficult to sit still in the waiting room of the hospital. I shouldn't be sitting here doing nothing, he thought, as he shifted his body to the end of the sofa. I should be out looking for Mala before she hurts someone else, but I can't. There is just no way in the world I could do anything until I know Beau is going to live. He saved my life! Why did he push me aside? Oh God, why wasn't it me that was shot?

He felt very uneasy and restless. Perhaps, he thought, it would be better to walk around, to work off this anxiety that he felt. He stood up, walked out of the waiting room, turned around and walked back in and sat down on the sofa again. The trouble was because of his heightened senses; whenever he walked through the hallways he would be sickened by the overwhelming smell of the chemicals used to sterilize the hospital.

So he stayed in the waiting room, while every nerve in his body seemed about to explode. He stayed and waited, and wondered about Beau's condition, and if Mala had been found. Everyone was looking for her. They were to call him when they had any news. He couldn't believe how it had all turned out. He leaned forward, elbows on his knees, as his head dropped into his hands. He sobbed ever so quietly, and thought, it should be me in that operating room not Beau, everyone knew that bullet was meant for me.

He wiped away the tears with the back of his hand, looked at his watch, and frowned when he saw it was almost two in the morning. Why is it taking so long? He has been in surgery for the last three hours. Dunbar didn't dare close his eyes, for he could still see the bullet hole and his friend's blood spilling out of it. The paramedic told him that Beau had only a fifty-fifty chance of survival.

Poor Beau, just when he found happiness this had to happen, Oh God please let him be all right, he thought, as he again lowered his head into his hand, and silently sobbed.

Janelle stood by the window of the waiting room, her arm in a sling, her forehead had a bandage to the right side of her eyebrow, and her head felt as if would explode. She admired the peaceful scene below the hospital window. The light from the street shone down on the magnolia petals that were floating in the soft breeze over the beautiful garden.

As she looked at the tranquil scene below, she wondered how it is possible to have experienced so much violence all in one day. Why? It's mind-boggling to think that someone, anyone, could deliberately hurt another person, especially someone as good as Beau. It hurt all the more because she knew the bullet was meant for her and that she should be the one in surgery, not Beau. Not him. He wouldn't hurt a fly. He doesn't deserve this pain.

She looked striking even though she was wearing a plain sweater that one of the nuns had loaned her, and her long curly red hair was half pinned up. Everyone has been very kind to her, but she felt miserable and wished it had happened to her. She just loved him so much, and once again the tears started to flow. I can't lose him now, as she dabbed her eyes with a tissue and rubbed her finger over her engagement ring. Not after the miracle of finding each other again after all those years of separation. Please God, she prayed let him be all right. Tears fell down her cheeks, as her body shook with quiet sobs.

Through the long night, various people stopped in to let the family know they were praying for Beau. Although New Orleans is a big city, word spread fast about the shooting. These were people that Beau had helped in one way or another. First it was Annie, a nurse who was off duty when she heard that Beau had been injured. She rushed back to work, to volunteer her services. She told Beau's mother, of the time her son, had been wrongly accused of a crime, and how Beau had proved his innocence. Annie took Rachel's hand, and said, "When he comes out of surgery, I will stay by his bedside until I know he is out of danger."

Rachel and Jonn thanked her, and asked Annie about her son, and how he was doing. "Oh, Annie said, didn't Beau tell you? He will be graduating next year from medical school. I thought you knew, but isn't that just like Beau not to talk about his helping us. Beau arranged for a private tutor to help my son obtain a scholarship for medical school. If it weren't for your son, mine would still be in jail, instead of a doctor. Speaking of doctors, I'm going to see what I could find out for you," she squeezed Rachel's hand and left the room.

Then Ancelet, the leader of a Cajun Clan, who had found himself unemployed when the oil fields stopped producing. He walked into the waiting room recognized Rachel, shook Jonn's hand, and said, "Beau helped me feed my family when I didn't have a job. If it hadn't been for him I don't know what we would have done. Your son helped me open a small Cajun restaurant, which is now very successful. I had to stop by to let you know how sad I felt when I heard he had been hurt. I know the waiting is awful, and I sort of thought that maybe you all might be a little hungry. Well, here," he pointed to his wife and one of his children who were setting up a buffet table, "I brought breakfast for now and sandwiches that you might want later."

"How kind of you," Jonn said shaking Ancelet's hand. "Now that I think about it, I guess we could all use a little food."

"My prayers are with him," Ancelet said as he and his family left the room.

And so it went, one after another came into the waiting room to tell how Beau had touched their lives.

Rachel insisted that everyone have something to eat whether they were hungry or not. It gave her something to do. Janelle had admired her so much for her kindness and her strength, but she could see that Rachel had begun to crumble.

Beau's parents were sitting on the sofa closest to the door. Jonn had his arm around his wife trying to console her.

"He will be fine. Now you know in your heart that he will. Don't cry. Here, sip the tea that I prepared for you. It's your favorite Rachel, apple cinnamon. You know you like that." He pulled a tissue out of his pocket, and said, "Let me wipe your tears. There now drink your tea and you'll feel better. You know God is listening to our prayers. Beau is going to be fine, wait and see." Then in a very serious tone, with his head bent, he whispered, "He has to be all right."

Janelle watched the couple consoling each other and felt like her heart was breaking. She saw Jonn trying so hard to be strong for his wife, and yet, so tender as he wiped away her tears.

Angele and Etienne entered the waiting room. Angele walked over to Janelle, and hugged her. "How do you feel?" she asked.

"Oh Angele, I'm so glad you're here," Janelle said as a sob escaped her throat. "I'm so worried about Beau. He's been in surgery for a long time."

Angele said, "Shh, don't cry. The news from Shabante is that everything will be just fine now. She says the bad time is over, Beau will recover."

Janelle nodded, and said, "Yes, I feel it too."

Etienne stopped by Beau's parents, shook hands with Jonn and said, "I heard what happened. I always knew that crazy Mala was trouble," he said trying hard to hold back the tears. "How long has he been in surgery? Does anyone know how he is doing?"

"It's been over four hours now, Etienne. I wish someone would tell us something. This waiting is killing us all." Jonn said as he rubbed his temples.

"I know the waiting is the hardest part. Oh I just don't understand life at all. It just doesn't make sense to me. How, could someone as good as Beau be wounded? Why couldn't this bullet miss him and wind up in a picture frame or a wall, why into Beau?"

"Etienne sweetheart," said Rachel between her tears. "I've known you since the day you were born, that's true isn't it?"

"Yes ma'am," whispered Etienne.

"Ever since you learned how to talk you have questioned everything, from the stars in the sky to how the world turns, right?"

"Yes ma'am, I guess I always gave you a hard time." Said Etienne with a bowed head

The room was silent as everyone listened to Rachel's words. Angele smiled because she knew it was true. Etienne always asked why about everything. He constantly took apart toys and motors to see how they worked. He had the kind of curiosity that always needed to know why.

"We don't know why the bullet found its way into Beau's chest. We only know it had to be this way, and although we are all saddened by his pain, we must believe that this is Beau's fate."

Jonn had a look of admiration on his face. That's why I love her, he thought. She is not only beautiful, intelligent and caring, but always concerned about making others feel better

"I am convinced that God in his infinite wisdom has chosen him to do great things, Beau will not die, not yet. I believe his job here on earth is not quite finished."

"I feel each of you have played an important part in Beau's life. Etienne you are a true and loyal friend and you have both been there for each other all your lives."

Etienne smiled and said, "That's right Ms Rachel we have."

Rachel looked around the room and saw Dunbar hunched over with his head in his hands. "Dunbar," she said in a steady voice.

He looked up, with his dark face glistening with tears, "Yes Maam?"

"Dunbar you have assisted Beau countless times with your keen awareness of people. Your ability to see the truth in people's character, and not what they wish to show to the world, is a phenomenal gift; one that you would not have, if you hadn't experienced the pain of deafness as a child. This terrible experience that you endured has made you stronger and much more understanding to other humans then anyone I know."

"This too will be true for Beau, when he is healed. He will become stronger, for he then will be able to feel the pain of others, and help them cope. You see you can't serve humanity without empathy."

He wiped the tears from his face, smiled and said, "Thank you Ms Rachel, I needed those kind words."

"Oh and sweet Janelle," said Rachel as a look of love softened her face. "You are like a ray of sunshine that has entered into our lives, and we would find it impossible to go on living without your glow. My son only had to look into you eyes to recognize that you were his soul mate. Your sensitivity and gentleness toward others is a wonderful gift. You are the daughter that I have always prayed for."

Janelle walked over to her and kissed her on the cheek, "and you Rachel are the mother in law I have always dreamed of."

Rachel took her hand, stood and said, "So you see, we are all in this world together. Each one of us is of a different ethnic background and religion, but none of that matters; for the most important thing in life is that we all care deeply about each other."

She walked to the sideboard laden with food, fixed a plate for Etienne, and one for Angele. Bringing it to them, she said, "we are all here because Beau is injured, but even if it were anyone of us in that operating room this same little group would be sitting right here, praying for the recovery of the injured one. In other words, even though we are not related, we are all family. Life is worth living when wonderful friends surround you. Together we will survive this existence, with it's valleys and peaks."

Janelle smiled and said, "Why that sounds like a recipe for life."

Angele was standing by the window munching on a shrimp salad, when she looked out at the view and noticed that it had snowed. "Look," said Angele, "it has snowed. You know it's the sign of a new beginning, the Choctaw Indians would call it a cleansing."

Everyone came to the window to see newly fallen snow, a rare sight in New Orleans.

"I just realized something," said Dunbar, "it's Christmas Day."

The door opened and Dr Alaya entered, he took Rachel's hand in his and said, "Beau is going to be fine. Annie is with him now, fussing over him like an old mother hen."

"I could not have asked for a more wonderful Christmas present then this," whispered Janelle to Angele, as tears of joy slid down her cheeks.

"Didn't I tell you everything would be just fine," Angele said while handing a tissue to Janelle.

"There was some damage to the upper extremities of his body," said Dr. Alaya, "but we were able to repair it and he is in stable condition. Beau is conscious, and wants to see all of you. Please remember, make your visit short, he must rest."

You could hear a sigh of relief as everyone started to breathe easier. Together they walked into Beau's room, enlightened by Rachel's words, knowing each one of them counts in this world, and is loved by the others.

As they walked into Beau's room, the first rays of dawn came shinning through the window, making the long terrifying night just a fading memory.

Epilogue

Janelle set the pen down, and poured herself a cup of coffee. She wanted to write a letter to her friend the Duke, but so much had happened she just didn't know where to begin.

It seemed like only yesterday that Beau had been shot. Could it be three years had passed since that awful night? She sipped the coffee au lait, took a bite of the beignet, and started to reminiscence, and once again picked up the pen.

When Beau and I married, she wrote, I gave half of the Sandbox to Mary and Sally. A small share was also given to Pedro and his wife. Beau and I have made it a priority in our lives to visit them at least three times a year.

Lizzie and Percy spend one month every year in New Orleans. They have become part of our family, Beau and I love their visits.

Etienne and Angele have married and I am doing my best to teach her how to cook.

Mala went completely insane when she heard that Beau was still alive and that we had married. The doctors say her case is hopeless. Her mind had snapped, and she will spend the rest of her life locked up in a mental institution.

Tyler the Terrible is no longer terrible. He has made many visits to Tibet visiting the Dali Lama and has found religion. He has made restitution to all the families he had tried to destroy, and had contributed half a million dollars to various charities, especially the mentally ill.

Dunbar Jones has left the New Orleans Police and has started his own private investigation service. He is doing well, especially since he hired several deaf people who read lips to do surveillance work.

Jonn and Rachel are great and in good health. They are spoiling their grandson Jonn Beauaguart Jr. something awful. I don't know what they are going to do when Beau and I tell them tonight that a second grandchild is on the way.

Speaking of Beau, he did win the election and is now Congressman Rampart. I am proud to say that the bill he fought so hard for was passed. It definitely will help many people get an education so they can acquire jobs, ensuring them a better life.

All's well that ends well. I don't think life could get any better than this.

Stay well. Come visit soon, we miss you.

I have to go now it will be dinnertime soon, and there is a new recipe I am dying to try.

Love always,
Janelle

Recipe for Life

Right the wrongs of yesterday and begin again,
    fresh each day.
Be thankful for what you have and not focus on what you
    don't have.
Fill your life with creativity and knowledge.
When faced with adversity, slip into plan B.
Be PERSISTENT, it is the only way to succeed.
Surround yourself with intelligent good friends.
Laugh a lot, even at yourself.
Respect others and their property.
Compliment and praise loved ones and strangers.
Ask yourself how the world was a better place because
    you were there.
Love yourself and your neighbors.
Fulfill your destiny!

The End